MW00479812

Retu
The Long Walk Home

David Chown

Contents

Forward

It is over seventy years since the end of the 2nd World War. To the Germans it was year zero as the victorious allies divided their country up among themselves. To the millions of German prisoners taken by the Soviets, their war would not be over for many more years, as they weren't released until the mid 1950s. Of the three million or so who were captured, it is estimated that over a million never returned. Of those who did return, the majority just wanted to forget their ordeal and get on with their lives to make up for the lost years. But at times when they realised someone was genuinely interested, they often opened up and tell their tales of captivity, deprivation and humiliation.

Although Josef Holz is a fictitious character, his amazing journey home to Bavaria from Russia is taken from first-hand accounts re-told to me by German ex-prisoners over the four years I was in Germany in the British Army. It is a testament to all the German soldiers who were prisoners in the Soviet Union for so long, and returned safely to their homeland to tell their tale. Josef Holz exists through them and their survival.

My book begins with Josef Holz being released from a work camp near Kiev in the Ukraine and follows him on his amazing journey back to his beloved home in northern Bavaria, mostly on foot. It took him through the Ukraine, then part of the

Soviet Union, and on through Poland and East Germany to West Germany.

Returning after so many years was never going to be easy, not for Josef nor for those he had left behind. Many waiting wives, if they hadn't heard anything from their husbands after a few years, had them declared 'presumed dead' allowing them to re-marry and start new lives with new families. Others had returned to find their families had gone, lost in the chaos of the war, which had been a tremendous upheaval for Europe, where millions had been killed, fled or expelled to many different places.

The National Socialists had called the German people the Master Race, but as Josef Holz said, "They called us the Master Race, but that was a lie. I was just a farmer from Bavaria who didn't want to go to war. I just wanted to look after my family and farm my land, but I had no option. I was never in the Nazi party, and I never wanted to be a soldier. Miraculously, I survived the horrors of the war, and finally, against all odds, I came home from Russia to my home and family.

The Family Farmhouse

Copyright © 2017 David Chown

ISBN 9781521873892

Chapter One - A Kind of Freedom

"Get out! Get out!" shouted the Soviet guards, as Josef watched the huge wooden gates of the prison camp opening. He had been in Soviet prison camps since the end of the Second World War. Now the gates of the camp were open and a hundred or so prisoners were being released. He could hardly believe it. Was he really free at last?

It had seemed like any other day when Josef Holz, a German prisoner of war, woke up earlier that day in April 1955. It was still dark and nearly the start of another day, although every day seemed the same. Josef had been a prisoner of the Russians for ten years.

Once a strong, rugged, handsome man, he was now 41 years of age, thin and haggard who outwardly looked older than his years. As he lay in his bunk in his dirty rags, he thought back over the many years of his imprisonment. He had been captured in early May 1945 during the Battle of Berlin in an area known as Lichtenberg on the eastern side of the city in the last days of the war.

He knew he was lucky to have survived. The Russians hadn't taken many prisoners in those last, bloody days of battle.

It may have been the Battle of Berlin to the Soviets, but to Josef and his unit it was the Fight for Survival in Berlin. Prior to their capture, they had been holed up in the basement of a large department store for more than two days unable to show their faces on the surface due to the continuous bombardment they were under.

It wasn't fear that kept them underground, although they were all afraid; it was the intensity of the Soviet bombardment. They were brave men who had fought their way across Poland in 1939 and the Soviet Union in 1941. Hitler had said the invasion of the Soviet Union, code-named Barbarossa, would only have to have the Germans kick down the door and the whole rotten regime would come tumbling down. This seemed to be the case at first, but the Red Army fought back with great bravery and the original German goal, Moscow in four months, was never realized.

Most of Josef's unit had been at the nine hundred day siege of Leningrad, but they had finally lost the momentum and the siege had been broken by the Soviets in January 1943.

By this time, a thousand miles south in Stalingrad, the 6th German Army under von Paulus was losing that battle, finally surrendering on 2nd February 1943 with the loss of a quarter of a million German lives and 91,000 German prisoners being taken. Later in 1943, the greatest tank battle of all was fought and lost by the Germans at Kursk in the Soviet Union. Josef's head reeled when he considered the losses, and the things he had seen during the dreadful war. He knew, however, that after six years of war, his unit was totally battle-hardened.

Most had also been at the battle of the Seelow Heights as part of the 9th Army under General Busse, only days before their capture. That had been one of the last assaults on a large defensive position in the war. The Seelow Heights were also known as the Gates to Berlin. After the loss of the Heights, the road was clear for the Soviet forces, and it was only a matter of time before the end came for the forces defending Berlin.

Just before the battle they heard of the death of the American President Franklin D. Roosevelt. Everyone thought that finally the war would now be over, and that somehow Germany would be miraculously delivered from their evil enemy, the Soviets. But that didn't happen, and the war dragged on for another three weeks with thousands more deaths of soldiers and civilians.

When the end finally came, burly Russian soldiers had hauled Josef and his comrades from the ruins of the department store, as women were being dragged out of nearby cellars to be raped on the streets. Josef saw many civilians murdered by the conquering troops who seemed to be completely out of control. Young girls, old women all were fair game for the lusting soldiers who had a score to settle. Josef had never forgotten their screams. As the Russians said, "The Germans sowed the wind and are now harvesting the whirlwind." Josef heard later that the Soviet leader Stalin had given his troops three days to do as they liked in Berlin as a gift for taking the city.

One particular incident had haunted Josef for many years. He and the group of other prisoners, who had been captured with him, had been tied up and lead into a badly damaged kitchen in the basement of a ruined house to await their fate. As they crouched there on the floor, a bear of a man, a Russian soldier, dragged a young girl into the room, lifted her up and sat her on the edge of a large pine table that stood in the middle of the room. He pushed her back roughly onto the table and ripped her underwear off. He then dropped his trousers and entered her. Josef cast his eyes down knowing that he was helpless. The girl sobbed quietly as she was raped, the joint of her right index finger in her mouth as she tried to bear the pain.

Suddenly from outside, Josef had heard shouting and a woman ran into the room screaming that they had her daughter who was only fourteen. The Russians laughed at her and one took her by the waist and sat her next to her unfortunate daughter. She too was pushed backwards onto her back, her lower clothing removed and she was raped beside her daughter. But she, unlike her daughter, screamed obscenities all the time. She would not submit and other jeering soldiers had to hold her down.

When the soldier had finished with the daughter, her clothes were thrown back to her and she stood there, a hunched figure with her head cast down watching her mother's dreadful ordeal.

When the soldier finally finished with the mother, he pushed her off the table and she fell heavily onto the stone floor. She continued to scream at the soldier who had so violently raped her, glaring at him with hate in her eyes. He shouted something at her, but she continued to scream at him. He looked angry and went round behind her and shot her at point blank range in the neck. Her daughter, seeing what had happened to her mother, ran from the ruins into the street. Josef often wondered what had become of the poor girl.

Josef's bad dream was interrupted by the sound of whistles and screaming. He jumped from his bunk, arranged his clothes and ran from the hut to fall in line outside with all the other prisoners. There were more than a hundred of them in all.

The roll call followed. This took some time. Standing in the chill early morning air was difficult to endure, especially in the winter. Josef was clothed in rags, mostly taken from other prisoners when they died. He had recently acquired a heavy army coat from a worker who had died beside him. Josef had been in the right place at the right time, but he knew that when the better weather came if he left the coat behind in the hut, it would be stolen. Whatever the weather, he would have to keep the coat with him at all times.

When the roll call was over, another whistle sounded. The men turned automatically to the right and proceeded out of the main gate to the mine that was about a twenty-minute march away. At that time of year, the track was very muddy, although at other times it could be dry and dusty or thick with snow and ice.

Josef had been in this camp for a number of years. He couldn't remember exactly how many, but it seemed a long time to him. This was the third camp where he had been imprisoned during his time in Russia, and it was probably the worst. The weather, the food, the hard work in the mine seven days a week, were the worst he had ever suffered. He sometimes wondered how long he could go on. Once at the coalface, which was deep underground, it was always very hot and very dusty. There was nothing mechanical down there and everything was done by hand. There were enough prisoners for this to be possible. When a worker became too ill to work, another worker would replace him.

Breakfast was handed out once they were at the coalface and ready for work. Black bread, a type of oatmeal in water and as much water to drink, as they wanted. Water was never in short supply as in some places in the mine it ran down the walls and was collected to drink.

The drilling was by hand and the coal was then smashed with large sledgehammers. They filled wheelbarrows and ran them to a large wooden pallet that was some way off back along the tunnel. When the pallet was full, it was winched to the top and loaded onto waiting wagons. The prisoners performed this process all day in semi darkness.

Lunch lasted just fifteen minutes with black bread and weak soup. Before they left the mine at the end of the day, the final meal of the day was given to them.

This sometimes included a type of meat or what looked like meat, but Josef came to be grateful for the food. It was keeping him alive to go home one day. The march back to the camp was always difficult as the prisoners were so exhausted.

Josef always slept well and always woke up before the whistle was blown. It gave him time to collect his thoughts and be mentally ready for another hard day. Although he had become a seasoned soldier over the years, he was by nature a very gentle, reserved, somewhat shy man. The soldier image didn't fit him at all.

Although he feared the Russian soldiers, he also had a certain respect for them. They didn't really seem much different from him. He knew that the vast majority came from farming communities devastated by the war, a war started by the Germans. Josef thought he was protecting his country when his battalion invaded Poland and later Russia. He had spoken with many Russian prisoners taken by the Germans in the early years and he felt great empathy for them. He knew that a link existed between him and them. He also knew that the official line of the National Socialist government was that the Russians were sub-humans and should be annihilated along with all Slavs. Josef knew this was a lie to encourage the German soldiers to fight harder in order to realise Hitler's goal of world domination as soon as possible.

By the end of the war, there were more than three million German prisoners in the Soviet Union, and it was estimated that over a million of them died in captivity because the conditions were so horrendous. None of the prisoners ever expected to see their homes again. The majority of them had never wanted to go to war in the first place, but Hitler had seduced the nation into doing his evil will. He had deceived the German nation and most didn't realise it until it was too late, that they were being led into a terrible war. Most of the people hadn't wanted to fight a war. They had just wanted to stay home to work, bring up their families, and lead normal lives. The war had been a tragedy for them all. It had destroyed their cities and ruined their lives. It had brought Germany to its year zero.

After being dragged from that Berlin cellar, Josef had been badly treated like all the other prisoners.

A boot or a club with a rifle was never far away, and he expected to be shot at any moment. Yet his luck seemed to hold, and, although his journey into captivity had been hard, many hundreds of miles in appalling conditions with only a once a day distribution of water and black bread, it was just enough to keep him alive.

The first part of the journey to the prisoner-of-war camp was by open truck, the prisoners squashed in like cattle. One night the truck didn't stop at all, even to allow them to relieve themselves. They had to do this on board the truck as it sped along the bumpy roads until it finally arrived at Stettin. This once beautiful city was unrecognisable with rubble piled up everywhere. The sick prisoners were removed before the truck left Stettin for another three-day journey that ended in Königsberg in East Prussia. Josef never knew what happened to the prisoners who were deemed unfit to travel or injured and left behind in Stettin, but he had a good idea.

Königsberg, like Stettin, was a massive ruin. He couldn't believe or understand why the high command of the army had fought to the bitter end. Surely, when the end of the war was in sight, a truce should have been sought to save both life and property?

From Königsberg, they were transferred to open cattle cars attached to a steam train which departed soon after the prisoners were all aboard. Josef couldn't remember how long he was on that train which was constantly shunted into sidings to allow faster trains to pass. It was probably four days during which time they received no food or water and had to relieve themselves where they stood, as the doors were not opened once during that terrible journey. Finally they arrived in Kiev, capital of the Soviet Republic of Ukraine, from where they marched for many hours to the prison camp.

The prisoners had been told earlier of the suicide of Adolf Hitler in a bunker deep under the streets of Berlin in April 1945. He was pleased to hear the news if it were true. He heard later of the mass hangings of many of the National Socialist leaders after the war in Nuremberg. Of course Josef had no way of knowing whether this was retribution by the victors or their just desserts.

As a prisoner, he had worked in numerous coalmines in the Ukraine. He had worked fourteen hours a day, seven days a weeks. He pondered 'worked' – it hadn't been work! It had been slave labour. The summers were oppressively hot and the mines were even hotter while the winters were freezing and severe. During the long hot summer nights of his captivity he often remembered the days leading up to his call up in 1939 and the beginning of the long nightmare.

He came from the northeast of Bavaria and was used to the outdoor life on his farm. He loved the hills and mountains and the green fields of the

Fichtelgebirge that were his home. He had been called up just before the outbreak of the war in 1939. He thought that his job as a dairy farmer would spare him from military service but it was not to be. He received his call-up papers which simply ordered him to report at 11 o'clock to the Town Hall in München, his local administrative town, on the following Thursday. That was only a week after the letter arrived, and there was little time to contact the army to tell them of his profession so that he could sort things out and stay home with his wife and son to continue farming, and producing milk for the local population.

On the day he left, he packed a small case, dressed in his Sunday best suit, and prepared to leave. He stood at the front door, called to his wife Helma, who came running from the kitchen with tears in her eyes. "Please don't go," she pleaded.

"I have to. It's my duty. But don't worry. I am sure I can sort things out when I get to Münchberg. You know there are reserved occupations, and I think I come into that category."

Secretly, she didn't really believe him but she just hoped, as he did. "Well, let's pray you will be home for dinner tonight," she said holding out her two little white fists in front of her as a sign of good luck.

"I will if I can," he said reassuringly.

He put his arms around her and they kissed. He felt the warmth of her breath as they kissed. They stayed locked together for what seemed a long while, until she bravely withdrew from his arms.

"Go now quickly and hurry home. I will be waiting for you," adding with a smile, "it's pork chops tonight in sauerkraut." Tears ran down her face as she watched him go. When he got to the end of the lane, he turned, waved, and blew kisses to her.

Josef's journey on foot to Münchberg took him about an hour and thoughts raced through his mind as he walked towards the little town. How lucky he was to live in such a beautiful place, and what a happy life he had. He thought of Helma. They had been married for three wonderful years. They had met in Hof, a local town, and when he saw her for the first time it was love at first sight. He hadn't really shown much interest in women before, as he was so shy. His work had taken all his time, and he certainly hadn't had a women. But on seeing Helma, his emotions had been stirred like nothing else had ever stirred him before. He was smitten and didn't really know what to do, as he was not worldly in that way.

At first he was nervous and ill at ease with her. He didn't know what to say, and when he did finally pluck up the courage to speak, he stumbled and was nervous and tongue tied with embarrassment. He just gave up and smiled. He knew how to tend to the animals on the farm and drive a horse and cart, but in the ways of love and courtship, he seemed to be at a loss.

Luckily for him Helma was quite the opposite. She was an outgoing, confident girl who soon put Josef at his ease. She could see he was by nature a reserved, quiet, modest man, somewhat nervous and easily embarrassed in situations where he didn't feel comfortable. But she saw a beautiful man, a man she adored from the beginning. Of medium height, Josef had short, straight blond hair, high cheek bones and deep blue eyes set in a round, boyish face, bronzed by the sun.

"You don't have to say anything, Josef. Just be yourself. That is more than enough for me," she would say, running her fingers through his hair. "You are my angel," Josef just looked away shyly not knowing how to reply.

He realised he had been slow to show his feelings in the past, but Helma was able to nurture the feelings within him and finally he was able to express his love for her, both emotional and physical. He could hold her and they could make love – both of them for the first time. It had been beautiful for them, sharing everything together. They realised that this relationship would last forever. They were two of a kind or maybe if not two of a kind, then perhaps it was that they slotted together, a part of each other, drawing on each others strengths. They both knew almost from the start that they would be partners for life. They had been waiting for each other all their lives.

Helma often teased Josef and he didn't understand whether she was being serious or joking. The first time she visited his parents' farm in Grosslosnitz Josef had been out in the fields. This gave her time to chat with them. They confirmed that their son was rather shy and unsure of himself. Helma replied that she already knew that.

When he finally came inside, he welcomed her with a kiss. He was wearing a straw hat with a wide brim to shield his skin from the sun. When he kissed her, his hat fell off onto the floor. Helma had laughed and told him he looked like a butcher with that hat. He had looked sheepishly at her, at a loss what to say, but he never wore that hat again.

They were married soon after at the beautiful church in Sparneck with all their family and friends attending the very special day. The following year their first child; a son Siegfried, was born, and he became their pride and joy.

When Josef finally arrived in Münchberg, he remembered going straight to the Town Hall where he found most of the young men of the area had gathered. There were many emotional scenes in front of the main doors, and two guards dressed in black uniforms from the Gestapo, were stopping anyone from entering the building. Mothers, wives, girl-friends were all protesting at the way their men were being taken away from them to join an army they knew little about. Some were crying and hugging their loved ones, telling them not to go. Others shouted at the guards.

The men consoled their womenfolk saying they would not be away long – that if war did come, it would only be a short war and they would all be home again very soon, probably by Christmas. Josef knew that's what the men had said at the beginning of the First World War, and those men had been away for four years. He was glad Helma had not come to town with him to see him off. These scenes would have upset them both.

Suddenly the great oak doors of the town hall opened, and two guards in black uniforms came out and ordered the men to fall in and march into the building, which they did in a very undisciplined and disorderly way.

It seemed to Josef that all the soldiers did was bark out orders although none of the recruits really knew what to do. They were ordered to strip down to their underwear and await inspection. Josef thought it looked strange to see many of his neighbours stripped down like that. He suppressed a smile as he got into line.

As each man got to the front of the line, he had to individually approach the desk where two stern-faced orderlies in white jackets ordered them to turn around, facing the others in the line, and drop their pants. When it was Josef's turn, he approached the desk and did as he was told. He felt quite embarrassed to show himself to so many strangers. Only his beloved Helma had ever seen him like this. They looked at his back then told him to turn around and face them. They looked at him with disinterest and nodded their approval as he quickly pulled up his pants and moved on.

One of the soldiers dressed in a black uniform came his way, giving Josef the opportunity to address him. "Excuse me, Sir," he started, "I am a farmer. I produce milk for the whole of this area." Before he could complete what he wanted to say, he was pushed aside by the soldier who said:

"Well, you are not a farmer anymore. We will make you a soldier to fight for the Fuehrer and the Reich, so shut up and get back in line."

Josef tried to say more but was told to shut up again and roughly pushed back in line.

When the inspection was complete and the men had dressed, they were ordered outside to board the waiting trucks that took them to barracks near Bayreuth for a period of basic training. As the beautiful countryside passed by, Josef hoped it wouldn't be too long before he would be home again with his dear wife and son.

In fact, he didn't return home for months, and then it was only for a long weekend prior to the invasion of Poland, of which he had no prior knowledge. After that, he did not see his wife again for months. When he was able to get home on leave, it was because Helma had recently given birth to their second child, a son Herman.

He only had a few, idyllic days of compassionate leave with his wife and darling new baby before he had to report back to barracks, and within a few days he was sent straight to the Eastern Front.

Suddenly, as Josef pondered the past, a Russian guard came into the hut. There had been no whistle that morning, and Josef was still lying on his bunk dreaming.

"Get up! Get out! You are all free to leave. Go home. Get out now you German scum!" he shouted. Josef hurriedly put on his clothes, picked up his little bundle of possessions, and ran outside where he found the gates of the camp open.

"Get out!" shouted another guard, as he handed passes to the prisoners which showed in Russian and German that they had been prisoners of war and had now been released.

Josef and the others, more than a hundred in all, looked around at each other unsure what to do. Were they really free now? If they made a dash for the gates en masse would they all be machine-gunned in their backs?

If they were free what did that mean? Free to do what? They were hundreds of miles from home in a prisoner of war camp with no money, no food, and no proper clothing, in fact nothing. Perhaps this was part of their punishment. If you can make it, you are free to go home, but if you don't, you're dead. We don't need you any more; we don't care what happens to you all – so just get out!

Over the years Josef had grown to accept his imprisonment. After all, he had been on the losing side of the most evil regime in modern history. He could expect nothing more than to be killed or be enslaved for the rest of his life. Yet he had survived. At once his mind wandered back to his home and his wife and family whom he had left so suddenly in Sparneck, Bavaria, more than fifteen years before. Since the end of the war, there had been no contact between them, so he didn't know whether they were dead or alive. Had they survived the war? Did they still live in Sparneck? So many questions but all without answers.

Personally he knew as a soldier that he had done nothing wrong. His conscience was clear. He had fought like a good soldier. He had always hated the National Socialists whom he blamed for causing the war and taking him away from his beloved family. He was glad that he had never voted for them at any time. He had always thought that Adolf Hitler was an evil man, the worst leader Germany had ever had but like most Germans, he had kept his opinions to himself.

His conscience was clear, but he had been on the losing side of the war so had to pay the penalty. He had often seen the dreaded German security police mis-handling prisoners both German enemies-of -the -state as well as the foreign enemy, but he had looked away. He had heard the screams and seen the ill treatment and looked away. He wasn't proud of that, but he had survived. It was only later that he realised that the invasion of Russia had not been liberation, it had been annihilation and he had been a reluctant part of it.

It had been better not to see too much and thus survive to tell the tale than to stand up and be counted as an opponent of National Socialism and be murdered. His first responsibility was to his family, not his country. That's what he had always believed. He knew that some would not understand him, but he thought that one had to live in Germany in those days to understand the situation. Opposition to the Nazis was not an option if one wanted to survive. Many had tried and many had died.

Now more than ten years later, he still felt the same. He knew that Germany's tragedy had been that, by and large the whole German nation had looked away and those who hadn't had been eliminated or had fled the country. He realised too that many had acquiesced; it was their time in the limelight. They would have to pay later for the crimes they had committed in the name of the German people.

He had heard of the July 20th 1944, plot to kill Hitler but it had been a failure and many more brave German souls perished before the total destruction of his beloved homeland. Josef's eyes filled with tears as he looked out of the open gates of the camp and saw mile after mile of empty fields ahead. He could smell freedom.

The prisoners approached the camp's huge wooden gates, first walking, then as they got nearer the gates their walking turned to running as they charged forward cheering loudly as they left the camp behind them. Josef felt that he had been there for what seemed a lifetime. Perhaps at last he was free.

Once out of the gates, he saw a town on his right in the distance so turned and headed towards it, as did all the other freed prisoners. He half expected to hear a machine gun in the rear mowing them all down, but except for the cheering he heard nothing. They were really free.

On his back he carried with him all his worldly goods, his little bundle of treasures in a small cloth wrap. Most important of these was his wooden figure of the Madonna and Child that he had carved in the first years of his imprisonment. He also had a chess set he had made during his captivity. He loved chess and had spent many hours in deep thought in the evenings after work thinking of his next move. He was saddened that he was not able to take the board with him as it was too large.

The going was hard; his shoes were just wooden clogs wrapped in cloth. It was early spring and the sandy soil was wet, cold and slippery to walk on. It seemed to him that the further he walked the further the town moved away. He looked around at the ragged band of men all trudging with him towards the town. These had been the cream of the German Army in 1939. "Look at us now," he thought! "We are totally demoralised tramps!"

It took three hours to reach the first buildings of the town, by which time it was mid-day. The roads were all of mud and not a motor vehicle was in sight, just horse drawn carts minus their horses simply dumped and neglected, in a haphazard way. The houses were of timber construction and dilapidated, and the whole place smelt of animals and decay. The few people who were around were well-wrapped against the cold wind that blew from the east. They scurried about their business as though eager to complete their chores quickly and get back inside. The little town was now full of German ex-prisoners, not the most popular people to have around Josef thought.

He broke away from the other prisoners and walked down a muddy alleyway looking for people, hoping for some charity, although he was pessimistic that he would find any. He stopped outside a farmhouse where an old woman in black was milking a cow. Josef approached her and made signs with his hand to his mouth. The woman stopped what she was doing and burst up from her seat and began to scream "Germanski" at him. She picked up her stick that lay nearby and beat him around the head and shoulders. Josef screamed with pain and hastily ran off. He realised that this was only a kind of freedom and that survival was not going to be simple. Relying on the kindness of strangers might not be an option.

Chapter Two - A Lift to the Border

Josef hurried back down the lane in a lot of pain. Once back on the main street, he joined the other prisoners and walked for a while until he saw an old man wrapped in peasant clothes repairing a cart. Once again Josef stopped and made the hand movement toward his mouth and this time he seemed to be in luck. The peasant stopped what he was doing, looked up, and smiled at him.

Josef felt quite pleased with himself; the first smile he had seen for quite a long time. The peasant showed Josef some damage to his old cart and Josef was soon able to put it right for the old fellow.

Then the peasant led him by the arm into his little wooden house that looked derelict from the outside, but inside a wood fire was burning brightly and it was quite cosy. He beckoned Josef to sit down and warm himself. Josef dozed off and dreamed of home. He was wakened sometime later by the peasant tapping his arm and offering him a bowl of soup. Drinking the soup hastily, he felt the warmth pass through his entire body. When he finished the soup, the peasant threw him a blanket and Josef quickly fell asleep once more.

He didn't know how long he had slept but when he awoke, it was light. Although his shoulders and head still ached from the recent beating, he felt a lot better and was glad for the sleep. As he pondered his new position, the peasant came in with rye bread and two eggs on a plate and offered it to him. It was then that he realised that he must have slept all the last evening and night. He greedily ate his breakfast as the peasant stood by impatiently waiting for him to finish.

Josef ate quickly and when he was finished, the peasant took him outside. He harnessed his old horse and gestured for Josef to climb up onto the cart. They sat beside each other and drove to the local market, which was in the centre of the town. Josef noticed that all the houses needed a good coat of paint, which they hadn't seen for many a year. Where windows were broken, the empty panes had been covered in pieces of wood and sacking hung in many of the existing windows masquerading as curtains.

Josef couldn't help but notice the great poverty that existed in the town and thought about the invasion by the Germans in 1941. He felt shame and great sadness for these basically decent people who not only were very poor, but had endured years of occupation and deprivation by the Germans.

There weren't many people buying what was on offer in the square, and the faces of the people who were there looked dejected, for there was not much to be had in the market. It was more a place to meet up and chat than to buy and sell. There were a few potatoes, greens, some very small carrots and what looked like home-made vodka for sale as well as some thin horses in a pen, but there didn't seem to be any takers. Not a lot really for the customers who stood around in groups chatting.

Josef was surprised and curious to see a bear with a ring through its nose on a chain being provoked to dance and bow and clap. He didn't like to see this. Although he was a farmer, he didn't agree with exploiting animals in this way.

It was mid afternoon when they arrived back at the peasant's home. The peasant motioned for Josef to go round to the back of the little dwelling to a dilapidated shed that housed some cows. The peasant gave him a shovel and broom and indicated what was to be done. Josef got the picture and cleaned out the cowshed to the delight of the peasant who sat there beaming. After Josef had finished in the shed, he was shown the fence and front gate, the peasant handing him a box containing some ancient tools. Josef nodded his head and proceeded to repair the fence. By this time, it was getting dark and he was unable to finish the work.

That evening, by the light of only two candles, the peasant gave him more soup. This time it contained potatoes and bacon. It had been years since Josef had tasted bacon and he quickly ate the meal and washed it down with some vodka that the kindly peasant offered to him. For the moment, though he was content with his present situation, he was eager to move on as soon as possible. However, he was beginning to think that the peasant might by now have other ideas.

He slept well that night on a straw mattress near the fire and dreamed of the gates of the prison camp being opened and the prisoners pouring out. In his dream, he was playing chess and thought to himself that he couldn't leave until the game was over.

When he awoke, it was morning and already light. He felt for his little backpack and sure enough the chess set was still there as was the little wooden Madonna figure and the tatty picture of his wife and children, which he had kept with him during all of his captivity. The picture was his most treasured possession and he kissed it every day. He also carried a small piece of Russian coal that he considered lucky. He wished on the coal every day that one day his life would change and he could go home to his beloved family.

After breakfast, he was given more chores to carry out which, he didn't mind doing as he was being fed well, but he wanted to continue his journey home. He knew he had a long way to go and was already days behind the others who had been released with him.

When he tried to explained to the peasant his intensions the old man frowned and shouted

"Niet! You work for me, Germanski." Josef definitely understood his meaning. He also realised that his leaving would have to be an escape rather than a departure if he ever wanted to see the green fields and hills of Upper Franconia again.

The next day he was instructed to follow the peasant into the field behind the house. It was potato-planting time, and Josef was given a large basket of seed potatoes to sow.

The ground was clay and wet and it was hard for him to get the potatoes into the ground. It took all day to finish the task and his back felt like it was breaking whenever he stood up. Dinner and a happy-faced peasant were waiting for him when he went back into the house that evening.

"You good Germanski; you good," the peasant said slapping Josef on the back.

Josef slept well again that night after his exhausting day and a good evening meal of potatoes in soup and a sip of vodka. The next day he was tasked with painting the veranda and sawing wood which took him all day. After his evening meal of chicken stew, he feigned sleep. When he heard the peasant snoring, deep in sleep, Josef made his way out of the peasant's little house and with his little bag slung over his shoulder, he set off in a westerly direction. It was dark, and he knew he had to put some distance between himself and the peasant before dawn. He didn't want the peasant to come after him as that might mean big trouble for him.

He had been walking all night and it was just getting light, when he noticed a farm nearby and begged breakfast from the kindly farm folk. Although he couldn't understand Russian, they were friendly to him and made him very welcome. It was warm, and he sat at a scrubbed pine table where he was served black bread, fried eggs and some ham – a banquet for him. He showed his gratitude by giving each member of the hospitable family a hug, before going on his way. He thought to himself that all farming families were similar whether in Russia, Poland or Germany. They were usually welcoming, friendly and hospitable just like Josef and his family would be to strangers.

After saying his farewells to the friendly Russians, it wasn't long before he came upon a tarmac road that ran east and west. He turned left, which was to the west, and proceeded with the sun warm on his back. He thought of home, his wife Helma, and his sons Siegfried and Herman who would now be young men. Josef wondered how, if he ever made it home, they would take to him. Would they be glad to see him or would he be treated as an intruder? Josef thought a lot, perhaps he thought too much, but there was nothing else to do as he walked. The scenery was flat and quite boring; just open fields many not planted up, but allowed to run wild. In the distance were steep hills on either side.

During the afternoon, he saw a farm set back off the road so decided to try his luck again and ask for some food and drink there. When he arrived, the place seemed to be deserted. He sat on a bench outside the front door and waited. It was quiet, there was a light breeze blowing and the birds were singing. After a while, Josef became impatient and took a walk around the back of the house and saw three people working in a field about a half a mile away from the house. He walked towards them and called out loudly. They stopped what they were doing and looked up, waiting in silence as Josef approached them.

"Hallo! I am Josef and I am on my way home to Bavaria." None of the three spoke but one, a large, strong, bald-headed man approached him as Josef held out his hand to shake hands with the man.

Before he had time to realise what was going on, the man hit him with his fist in the stomach. Winded, Josef fell to his knees gasping for breath. The man roughly placed a rope around Josef's neck, and he was dragged back to the house on all fours. Once outside the front door, he was tied to a ring that hung from the wall and his hands were tied behind his back. The three peasants said something that Josef didn't understand then went into the house and shut the door.

Josef sat there, uncomfortably propped up against the wall. Every part of his body seemed to ache. After many hours, he started to yell out. "It is cold! Please help me. I am hungry and thirsty! Please help me," he called.

The door opened suddenly and out came the old lady who had earlier been working in the field. Without speaking, she kicked Josef really hard in the chest then shouted something before returning inside and slamming the door.

Josef stayed there all night tethered to the wall with a rope around his neck and his hands tied behind his back. He felt like a dog. By morning, he was cold and damp and wished that he could have died during the night. He sat there quietly waiting for someone to come out and help him, but no one came out of the building during the whole morning.

Around mid day, the door opened and a girl he guessed was the daughter, untied him from the wall and made him crawl across the yard on his hands and knees as she pulled him along on the lead that was still attached around his neck. She took him to the cowshed where Josef saw that there were six cows.

She connected him with a heavy chain, to an iron cow feeder. She clamped the chain to one of his ankles, and he screamed out in pain as she locked the padlock tightly to the chain. She then removed the rope from around his neck and released his hands that were tied behind his back. Without speaking to him she left the cowshed.

In the evening, the brute who had punched him in the stomach, came into the barn with a riding crop in his hand. He ripped Josef's shirt from his back and threw it to the ground. He beat Josef twice around the face with the riding crop and shouted something to him as Josef screamed out in pain.

The brute fitted a long chain onto Josef's ankle and showed him how to milk the cows, a job Josef already knew and did well. When Josef had finished, the brute gave him a quick smirk and took the fresh milk from the barn to the house. Once again, Josef was left on his own in the cold cow barn till the following morning when, after again milking the cows, he was given some black bread and a raw potato.

Before he could finish his meagre meal, the daughter came in carrying the dreaded riding crop and threatened Josef with it. She indicated that he should clean up the cow's droppings and put them in a tin bath that stood nearby. There was no shovel or spade so he had to collect it on his hands and knees in his hands. When he finished the cleaning, he was offered water from a bucket that he greedily drank.

He then washed his filthy hands in the water that was left in the bucket. That evening he was not offered anything to eat, and he felt as if he were starving to death.

After another awful night when he again thought that he would be better off dead than alive, the daughter arrived and offered him more bread after he had milked the cows. The daughter, a buxom young thing enjoyed teasing Josef, poking him with her crop and running it up and down his bare back. Josef half expected to be beaten but no beatings came from the girl who finally said that her name was Danuta.

In the evening, she came back with the bucket and indicated that he should milk the cows again. He complied and she took the milk away. Sometime later, she returned carrying a candle in a wooden holder that she placed on a shelf above Josef's head. She indicated that he should lie down on his back on the cold, wet floor, which made him shiver. She then began to run her crop up and down his chest. This gave him goose bumps. He became aware that she was undoing the buttons of his trousers, which she slowly removed. As he lay there on the damp floor without any clothes, her hands began to greedily caress his body all over, massaging, stroking, pulling, feeling, and pinching him all the while grunting some words that he could not understand.

He watched her as she stood up, lifted her dress and removed her under clothing. Understanding the situation, Josef stopped her. "No, no," he said, and indicated that she should unlock his chain so that he might perform better. She understood his meaning, smiled and went to fetch the key from a hook above the barn door to undo his padlock.

He remained lying on the cold floor as she nervously undid the padlock and then continued feeling his body as she began to shake with excitement. With the chain removed from his sore ankle, he stood up and stretched. He stroked her dark hair as she knelt in front of him eager to begin. "I am sorry, Danuta," he said under his breath, as with one almighty punch to her face, he knocked the poor girl out.

He quickly dressed, chained up the unfortunate girl as he had been chained, and replaced the key on the hook above the door. He then stumbled off as rapidly as he could in the dark, walking down the dirt track and turning west. He struggled on all through the night. As it got light, he saw that there was a stream by the road. Stopping for a while, he washed as best he could and continued walking as fast as his tired legs would take him.

Around late morning, a truck full of Russian soldiers pulled up alongside him, "You want a lift comrade?" Josef nodded that he did.

"Germanski?" they enquired.

"Yes, Germanski," he said.

"Get in. We help you get to Germany."

"How long you are in Russia?" they asked.

"Ten years," Josef replied and added, "Russia very nice place."

"You stay ten years? Yes? You think Russia very, very nice place." They said laughing.

The young Russian soldiers explained to Josef as best they could that they were on their way to Poland to a new posting. "We like Poland." one told him. Another said, "Poland is Russian. We are bosses in Poland."

Josef let the limited conversation go. He thought it better to be quiet and just watch the flat, boring Ukrainian countryside roll by. It was not beautiful like his Bavaria, but it looked peaceful and very rural. As they drove through the many small villages, the people seemed afraid to look at their vehicle. They looked away as though they hadn't seen it. An air of fear pervaded the people.

As he sat there on the floor of the truck, his mind returned to the day he had been wounded in Russia. He remembered the burning shrapnel entering his thigh, falling down and drifting in and out of consciousness as he was moved to a field hospital some miles behind the lines. This would have been towards the end of 1943 when the successes of the past on the Eastern Front were turning to defeats for the Germans. The field hospital was a large marquee filled with bodies and blood.

His recovery was slow as his wounds had become infected, the result of not being treated immediately. On the day of his injury, dozens of other soldiers had been killed and injured due to the fierce Russian advances. Josef thought that the Germans seemed to be in retreat.

Josef sensed that the Germans were losing the Russian campaign. He, along with thousands of other soldiers, had looked to a negotiated settlement of the war and a quick return to their families. As it was, he had been injured and didn't know how long he would be in this place recovering. In fact, it was three weeks before he returned to his unit where the fighting was getting worse and the casualties getting heavier. He was also aware that many of the old faces, his friends, were gone.

At times, he prayed. However, he felt that he had been forsaken and forgotten by an unforgiving God in an unforgiving land at a time when his life was in the greatest danger. Still he prayed that one day the war would end and he could return to his family – to Helma, Siegfried and Herman and his beloved Bavaria.

He was suddenly returned to the present by a prod from one of the young Russian soldiers who told him that they were nearing the border with Poland. They had driven for many hours while Josef had been lost deep in thought.

They dropped him off some distance west of the town of Krakovets telling him he would need to walk from there to the village of Korczowa, a few minutes away which was over the border in Poland. They wished him good luck as he got out of the truck. He watched the truck as it sped off westwards with the soldiers waving to him.

He saw that when the vehicle reached the border they just drove straight over without stopping to speak to any of the border guards on either the Russian or Polish sides. He wondered why he couldn't have just stayed in the truck and driven with them into Poland. He couldn't have known that had the soldiers been found smuggling people over the border, they would have received severe penalties.

These young Russian soldiers had no hatred of the Germans and had done him a great kindness. Indeed, some would see service in East Germany in the future if they were really lucky. It was their parents who hated the Germans! It was the older generation who had suffered so badly from the war.

Chapter Three - The Long Dark Night

Josef saw the Polish border just ahead. He felt some apprehension about entering the country. He knew that the Poles had suffered badly under the German occupation, and he had seen this first hand in 1939 when Germany invaded Poland. Now the tables were turned and the Poles were certainly no friends of any Hun. He remembered hearing about the SS in Lodz and how they had treated the local population, especially the Jews, with total contempt and much brutality. He knew that the country had been devastated by six years of war. It was still under the military rule of the Russians for which many blamed the Germans directly, although they couldn't voice these views. Josef wondered why, when the Poles had been on the winning side, they were still occupied by the Russians?

The little booth was on the far side of the crossing point, and there was a red and white bar across the road that could be raised and lowered on both sides of the border. Josef got out the pass that he had been issued showing he had been released recently from a Russian prison camp. The Russian guards looked at the paper disinterestedly and waived him on into Poland.

There was no traffic on the road as he slowly walked towards two Polish guards who were waiting for him in front of their booth, as he approached. As he came up to them, he showed his pass for them to inspect. The guards looked at each other then looked at him and began to shout. He couldn't understand a word they were saying, but he knew they were not pleased to see him.

They grabbed him by his rough prison shirt collar, twisted it until he nearly choked, then bundled him around the back into what looked like a huge metal container behind their booth. He was pushed in with a heavy shove to his right shoulder and a hard kick to his backside. The metal door clanged closed behind him and he was left in total darkness.

He felt his way around in the container and sat down on the damp, cold, metal floor with his back propped up against the cold metal wall. He shut his eyes hoping that when he opened them all would be ok and that it would be light. But he was only fooling himself and this didn't happen.

As he sat in misery, his mind travelled back in time to when the German Field Police suspected that he had refused to fire on the enemy, and had arrested him. This incident had come about when, in discussion with other soldiers of his unit over a beer, they had talked of the hypothetical situation that if they were ordered to shoot defenceless women and children, would they refuse to do so? Most had said they would obey the order, but Josef had said that he wouldn't be able to do so. Somehow this had been brought to the attention of his commander who had in turn reported him to the Field Police, and he had been arrested.

He was questioned for several hours and was then held in solitary confinement for many hours. He was told it was his duty to obey all legitimate orders given to him by senior NCO's and officers. If he thought they were wrong he could complain later, but at the time the order was given, he had to obey without question. He was told that in times of war soldiers of the Wehrmacht could be shot for disobeying an order. He was a soldier of the Reich, and it wasn't for him to pick and choose which orders he should or shouldn't obey.

Realising it would be dangerous for him to disagree, and in order to secure his early release, he had given the Field Police his assurance that it had all been a mistake and he would obey all orders given to him at all times. There was no point in arguing that something may be wrong with this policy. He had his own opinions but realised he had been foolish to voice them. He knew, however, in his heart of hearts that he would not be able to blindly obey all orders.

Some months later, he remembered being ordered to take a Russian prisoner into the forest near where they were billeted. "Get rid of him! We are not taking prisoners," an officer barked. Josef didn't know the officer but he obeyed the command.

He had cocked his rifle and indicated to the terrified prisoner, who was shaking violently, that he should walk ahead of him into the forest. They walked for some ten minutes into the dense undergrowth until Josef shouted for the prisoner to halt.

The Russian was shaking like the leaves of the trees above him when he turned to face his executioner. He fell on his knees praying and begging to be spared. Josef stood back and faced his terrified prisoner. They looked into each other's eyes. The Russian then shut his eyes and prayed out loud awaiting his fate. Moments later a single shot rang out from Josef's rifle. There was a long silence. The prisoner opened one eye then the other, and looked at Josef questioningly.

Josef had fired into the air. He looked at his prisoner and indicated with the end of his rifle that he should now disappear. The Russian stood up and they eyed each other suspiciously. The prisoner bowed and mouthed the word "comrade" as he put his hand on Josef's shoulder and with a slight smile on his face, turned and ran. Josef returned to his unit and nothing more was said of the incident. Josef had proved to himself that he could not obey all orders without question.

And now here he was once again the prisoner. After more than ten years of being a prisoner of the Russians, he was now a prisoner of the Poles. The time he spent in the darkness of that container was probably the worst experience of his life. He was in total darkness; at times he felt as if he were passing out, and at others as if he were drowning in a sea of black. He breathed deeply, but this didn't help. When he tried to stand, he collapsed. The sheer panic of claustrophobia took over and his whole body shook uncontrollably as his breathing became short and fast. He thought that he was having a heart attack and was dying. Instead, he began to weep and scream and bang on the side of the container. He fell down on the damp, cold floor of the container and finally passed out.

What seemed like many hours passed in the damp blackness of that container, as he drifted in and out of consciousness before the metal doors were at last opened, and he heard the shouts from the guards. He tried to stand up but his legs gave way under him. He shielded his eyes as he attempted to focus on the guards and get used to the light again, but this also was hard to do.

Before he could come to his senses, buckets of icy water were thrown over him as he lay on the floor of the container. The guards beat and kicked him as they dragged him out of the container by his ankles. He rolled into a ball to protect himself as best he could from the violent attack. The kicking seemed to go on for a long time before he felt a resounding crack from a rifle butt to the side of his face. He screamed out in pain and began to sob, wishing that the guards would finish him off there and then. But they didn't. Instead they shouted, "Master Race! Master Race! Vermin! Get out of here, you scum."

Josef struggled to his feet and hobbled off carrying his little bag as fast as he could away from the checkpoint, blood oozing from his neck and right ear. He was free, and he knew that he had to get away and put some distance between himself and his captors as quickly as he could. He painfully limped away from the checkpoint, away from such hatred and violence. So this was Poland? He hadn't expected a welcome, but neither did he expect to be beaten and imprisoned.

Ahead he saw a forest where he thought he would be able to lose himself for awhile to recover. It was an effort to get to the forest, as it was further away than it looked. It was uphill all the way with ditches to cross and hedges to crawl through. He had to use every bit of his strength that he had left.

Finally, after about an hour, he was safely in the forest. As he sat at the base of a tree, he tried to tend to his injuries by patting the blood on his neck and ear with large fern leaves, which grew in profusion under the trees. It hurt like hell but at least the blood had dried a bit to seal the wounds. He was soaking wet and every part of his body ached. He took off his shirt and hung it on a branch of a tree hoping it would dry in the little patch of sun filtering through the trees above him.

As he sat there on his own, he became aware of the sound of voices and rustling leaves nearby. Soon, he saw unkempt figures approaching him as if from nowhere. He was surprised to see some of the other German prisoners who had been released at the same time as himself coming towards him. They looked like zombies with big staring eyes. In one respect, he was glad to see them and was glad for the company. Generally, however he would rather have made his own way home and not be with a band of ex- German prisoners who might look threatening when travelling in a group.

Stumbling up to Josef and seeing the bad shape he was in, one of the group offered him some black bread, which Josef consumed ravenously. He hadn't eaten for days and when he considered it, he couldn't remember when he had last eaten. But then he didn't even know the time or what day it was. Such information was irrelevant to him. What he did know was that he was still alive and wanted to survive to see his family again.

He told the others of the beatings and imprisonment he had received from the guards at the border. They all said that they had not been treated badly, but maybe it was because they were twelve ex-prisoners and there were only two guards on the border.

"Strength in numbers," somebody commented.

Josef realised he had been naïve to think that he could just walk home with no consideration for the past. Recent history had been hard on Central Europe. He would have been quite happy to forget the past, like indeed the whole of the German nation, but many of their neighbours were not so forgiving or forgetful.

When he had eaten, the group asked him what he was going to do? He told them that he would prefer to stay with them for the time being; after all they had the food! The others laughed and they sat there for some time discussing their options. Should they continue immediately or take a break for Josef to recover? They decided to take a break and start out afresh the following morning. Glad to be together, the group rested and exchanged stories and thoughts of their journey to that point.

Someone said that it was the 1st World War that had sown the seeds of the rise of National Socialism that led to the Second World War, but Josef found it hard to understand how the Nazis had flourished so quickly. He knew that initially they had led the German people into believing that a vote for Hitler would be a vote for full employment and a better standard of living. Germany would once again be able to hold its head up high after the humiliation of Versailles. It was only when the war started that they realised that they had been seduced and mislead by their leaders and especially Adolf Hitler. By then it was too late to stop the Armageddon that was to come.

There were many views on the subject, but even in this situation Josef was cautious to not give his opinion too openly. He wasn't a politician; he was a farmer from Bavaria. Even so, these were questions that he sometimes thought about but didn't comment on so long after the war. What he did know was that he had never been a member of the Nazi party nor had any of the others in his unit. They were all there because they had not been given a choice. They had been conscripted and as patriotic Germans, they had answered the call of duty. Not doing so was never an option.

They all found places to sleep close to each other in the woods before the next stage of their journey. Josef found it difficult to sleep that night as he listened to the howling of the wolves that roamed the forests in packs. Whether they would attack humans he wasn't sure, but the sound was spine chilling and unsettling.

When sleep finally did catch up with him, he dreamt of the Reichstag Fire in 1933 when he was just sixteen years of age. He remembered it well. His father thought it was an outrage. "It's the Communists," he had shouted. His father always thought everything bad was the fault of the Communists. In fact, a hapless twenty-five year old Dutchman, named van der Lubbe, said to be a Communist, was accused and later executed for the fire. The night of the Reichstag fire was the night democracy finally died in Germany.

Josef often thought of his father and mother and his childhood. Times had been good and he looked back on them with great affection. They were poor, but everyone around them was the same, so it was normal. They were a normal family living in abnormal times. But were there ever "normal" times?

He remembered the peasants in the villages who had retreated into their hovels as the German troops approached during the invasion of Poland and Russia. To them, there wasn't much difference between the Soviets and the Germans. Both came to steal their food and rape their women. The rural villagers really were on their own. They had no radios and there was little or no contact with outsiders, which made them fiercely independent. It was probably only their homemade vodka that sustained them. Josef's early life had been far better with many friends and neighbours and many small towns nearby to visit. The life of the rural Poles and Russians was a world away from his own.

He also often thought of the cold winters when he was a child. The best place to be was always in bed under the enormous feather quilt that had belonged to his grandmother before she died. People inherited things like that in those days before the war. As a boy in winter, when he undressed at night, he always put his clothes in the bed beside him so that they would be warm the next morning. And in the morning, as it became light, he used to wonder at the ice on the inside of the window making strange patterns that fascinated his young mind. From his warm bed, he remembered the noises downstairs of his mother making the fire in the kitchen directly below his bedroom. He waited for her to knock on a water pipe that ran from the kitchen, up through his bedroom to the loft. This told him that it was time to get up and get ready for the day, and perhaps more importantly to him, that his breakfast was ready.

During the severe winter months, by the time he got downstairs the kitchen would be warm with the wood stove blazing away, the smell of bread rolls warming on top, and the aroma of freshly-made coffee giving off a homely feel to the kitchen. It had been an idyllic childhood, and he always had a great feeling of security being with his parents even though they were both strict and always expected his total obedience. So many memories flooded his mind, all good memories that had been ripped away from him by the advent of the war.

Chapter Four - No Fish Tonight Then?

Josef woke up the next morning at first light to the deafening sound of birds. It was the dawn chorus and it seemed much too loud for him to sleep. He jumped up and woke the rest of the group who all seemed to be sleeping through it. They protested and swore at him for waking them so early.

"How can you sleep?" he asked. "The birds are so loud. Come on! We need to leave." Reluctantly, they gathered up their few possessions and before long, were all back on the road. It was a damp and misty morning and there was heavy dew on the trees, as they trudged along the empty road. They couldn't see too far ahead because of the mist, but after a short while they saw a road sign pointing west for Krakow, Wroclaw and Warsaw. This was the direction they decided to follow as it was in a westerly direction. Everything worth living for was in the west. Everything behind them had been one long nightmare.

It was a fine day, and after a few minutes walking, Josef felt better. His body didn't ache anymore and he knew he was now, once again, on his way home.

As they walked, another of the party whom Josef only knew vaguely moved up beside him and walked with him. He introduced himself as Albrecht.

"I am from Essen in the Ruhr. Do you know it?" he asked enthusiastically.

"No, I have never been there. Is it a nice place?" Josef asked.

"It was a good place to live, lots of work. Coal mining, you know! Excuse me, but I don't know your name?" he asked.

"I am Josef Holz from Bavaria – the Fichtelgebirge," he replied adding, "Were you wounded in the war?"

"No, I was lucky. We lost most of our original unit though. It was terrible. Such a waste of life, and for what? Just sand. I was in North Africa with Rommel you know," he told Josef with some pride in his voice.

As they walked on together, Josef asked his companion what he had done before the war, before he was called up.

"I was a miner, of course. Most of the men in our town were miners. That was awful work down there digging for coal. I hated it, but there was nothing else in the town. When the call came, I thought the army would make a great life. Anything was better than down the mine." He thought for a moment and added. "I thought the army would be exciting and I would see many new lands. Well, it was all those things but not in the way I had expected. It ruined my life, I can tell you."

"The war ruined all our lives," Josef added in confirmation. Suddenly Albrecht began to speak again, but in a whisper.

"Do you know, I am 36 years old and I have never had a woman? I am so ashamed," he confessed. He looked at Josef as they walked together and continued, "I was a soldier, but I have never been a man."

As they walked side by side, Josef could hear his partner sniffing. His confession had made Albrecht feel emotional, and Josef looked round to see that Albrecht was crying silently.

"We are on our way home, Albrecht. All that will change for you. You will meet a wonderful woman, get married and have lots of children. I am sure of it."

Albrecht was quiet for a long time as they walked together. After a while, in a broken voice he said, "I hope so, I hope so. Otherwise what has all this been for? I don't know even if I have any family left in Essen. My mother, my father, my sisters, perhaps there is no one left. Maybe they were all killed in the bombing." Albrecht trailed off his sentence and left the main party and disappeared into the woods.

Josef followed him a few moments later, to make sure that his comrade was ok. He found Albrecht sitting on the stump of a tree with his hands over his eyes, weeping like a baby. Josef approached him, knelt down in front of him and put his arms around his comrade's neck.

"Albrecht, you will be ok. You are a survivor like all of us here. You survived the war, and the camps in Russia. Now you are on your way home. We are a little team here.

We care about each other, don't we? And we care about you. So come on! Let's get going. Let's get home." Josef stepped back a pace as Albrecht stood up and dried his eyes with the backs of his grubby hands. He looked Josef in the eye and thanked him for his concern.

"You are a good man, Josef. I will survive, but for what? I don't know the answer to that, so my future is still in doubt. I hope I find that my family has survived and everything will just carry on as it was." He thought for a moment and continued, "Well I wouldn't go down the mines again, that's for sure! I am finished with digging coal. I will need to find something else above ground." Josef nodded but didn't answer.

They returned to the main party and Albrecht told Josef he felt a lot better. "We went to North Africa to support the Italians in May 1942," continuing his story. "They had been routed by the Tommies in the Western Desert. During 1942, we had some victories. I was attached to an anti-tank unit. I was there over a year but my unit left just before the surrender of the Africa Corps in 1943. Do you know," he sighed "there are over 18,000 German soldiers buried in North Africa?" Albrecht added. "And the Tommies? They took 130,000 prisoners. What a dreadful waste?"

"My unit was transferred to Italy," he continued. "We fought our way from the south to the north of the country. Then we went to Paderborn in Westphalia to reorganise. Later I was posted to Northern France when the invasion across the Channel came. Then it was just a case of being pushed back all the time, although," he added after some thought, "We all fought really hard. It certainly wasn't a walkover, but we were overwhelmingly out numbered by the other side. In spite of this, in mid -December 1944, the Americans were totally surprised by our attack in the Ardennes. It caught them off guard. Do you know about it?" he asked Josef.

Josef nodded his head. "The Allies weren't prepared for a counter attack in mid-winter," Albrecht continued. "There was thick snow and it was freezing. When it was obvious we could not win against such odds in late January 1945, my unit was moved to the Eastern Front, and that was it for me. I was only there a few weeks before I was taken prisoner. I survived the war but, like you, was a prisoner of the Russians for ten years.

That was it, my life seemed over." Josef stayed silent. He just listened.

As they walked, Josef noticed that the road ahead followed a stream that meandered over the flat waterlogged land. He beckoned to the others, "Come on! Let's take a short cut across the fields." They followed him in a westerly direction expecting to meet up again with the road a few miles further on, and maybe cutting out a lot of walking. The detour was farther than they thought and after walking for about an hour over the boggy fields, they found themselves in a heavily wooded area.

"This doesn't seem much of a short cut," someone said to Josef.

He had to agree. As he led the party through dense undergrowth, Josef was a little ahead of the main party. Suddenly, as he pushed ahead, he felt the earth disappear from under him as he went over the edge of a ravine that he hadn't seen. He fell about twenty metres to the bottom, where he landed heavily on his feet that buckled under him. He heard a crack as a bone in his left knee broke, and he laid on his back in agony on the damp Polish soil.

It took the others quite a while to reach him, as they clambered down the steep embankment of what seems to have been a disused open mine. Seeing Josef lying still at the bottom, they thought he must be seriously injured. All this time, Josef drifted in and out of consciousness due to the intense pain.

When the group reached him, they stood over him wondering what to do. Josef tried to talk as everyone kept asking how he felt. Finally one of their number known as 'the doc' knelt down to examine Josef's leg. He felt it, was silent for a long moment then felt it again. Josef screamed out to be left alone. He would die there where he lay; he knew it!

The doc continued to examine his legs for some while before saying, "You will be pleased to know, Josef, that I don't think either of your legs are broken, although one seems to have a dislocated bone. Don't worry! I'm sure I can fix it for you. I'm good at this sort of thing." Josef was not re-assured as the pain was unbearable.

The doc found a short piece of stick. "Here, Josef, bite on this stick," he said, handing it to Josef. "Just think of home."

Josef did as he was told, as he had no other option. He felt the doc's hands moving up and down his leg. Then suddenly he heard a loud crack as the doc applied pressure to his right knee and the bone clicked back into its correct position.

Instantly, he felt pain as he had never felt pain before. It started from his leg and worked its way upward and downward until his entire body was overwhelmed with pain. He screamed out and the whole forest was engulfed in the sound of his agony.

"Lie still for a moment Josef. The pain will soon go," the doc assured him. Unable to do anything else anyway, he just lay there in desperate misery.

Josef drifted in and out of consciousness, for how long he didn't know, but after awhile the pain did begin to ease. The others put together a stretcher from timber that was lying around and within a couple of hours of the accident they were once again on their way. It wasn't long before they found the main road again and decided there and then that they would not make any other detours. They would stick to the roads.

The detour had been a costly mistake for the party. Not only had they lost much time, but also Josef could have been seriously hurt. Luckily, his injury would not be permanent although he was still in terrible pain.

They walked for some while carrying Josef on the stretcher, all chatting about their hopes for the future and their chances of getting home and, of course, Josef's fall, which all agreed was just bad luck that he had been leading. Having walked for a good way, they stopped by the roadside to rest. Some of them left the party to relieve themselves.

Josef nodded off as the mid-morning sun warmed his face.

As usual, he began to think, and to make plans for when he got home, how he would expand the farm, what crops would be needed to feed the people, like corn, wheat, barley and hops for beer and schnapps, big in Bavaria. He also wanted to take his family on holiday to the Alps, Oberammergau or perhaps Vienna. Vienna would be wonderful, as he had spent a romantic holiday there before the war with his wife and young son Siegfried. It would be very special to return as a family. He longed to get to know them again and to give his sons a father that he hoped they needed and had longed for. They were the most important things in his life. His thoughts were endless.

Lying on his makeshift bed, his mind wandered back to the last time he was in Vienna. He had seen Hitler on the balcony of the Hofburg Palace and later in the day on the balcony of the Hotel Imperial near the Opera House. That would have been in March 1938. It was just after the Anschluss, the union of Germany with Austria. He remembered being struck by the insignificance of the little man who was the leader of the German people. He didn't realise how this evil man would one day totally change and ruin his life and the lives of the whole German nation. Neither did he realise how this one man would lie to the German people, telling them they needed to go to war to protect their borders from those who would supposedly threaten them. Or how the German army would invade most of Europe causing chaos and hatred by all who were occupied, and finally how the war would bring the German nation to total defeat.

He thought of his dear wife Helma and her favourite flowers. She loved gladioli and he decided he would plant a whole bed of them just for her when he got home. He would plant some every week during the spring to ensure a whole summer of her flowers.

Suddenly he was woken from his sleep by Dieter Scholz, his good friend in the group.

"Hey, look what I have found, Josef?" he called. A handsome, athletic-looking man from Munich, Dieter was in his early 40s, tall, lean, and blond. They had met during their basic training in Bayreuth and had become good friends. Josef looked round and saw that Dieter was carrying a stick grenade. He looked closer and identified it as of German origin, a Mark 24. They had both learned to use these grenades years before, but this one looked old, damp and corroded. Dieter undid the base cap in the hollow handle and saw a porcelain ball attached to a string drop out.

"Take it easy, Dieter," Josef said. "Don't pull on that cord or we'll all go up."

Dieter laughed, "Don't worry! We were trained in them, remember? I know what I am doing!"

Nearby was a lake and Dieter remembered something he had seen other soldiers do during the war in Russia. "You pull the cord and throw the grenade into the lake," he explained. "It explodes and up come the dead fish, maybe loads of them. Supper for us all," he said smiling hopefully.

They all went to the lake. "Stand back!" Dieter ordered, as he went to the edge. After he pulled the cord, he would have five seconds to throw the grenade before it exploded. Josef commented that it looked so old it probably wouldn't work. Others, who were standing nearby, said that it was so old it might explode at any moment. The group all moved back and held their breath. Dieter pulled the cord.

Before he had time to throw the grenade, there was a huge explosion. Dieter's body took the full force of the explosion in his face and chest. He was blown upwards and backwards falling heavily to the ground screaming, his face and chest covered in blood. Josef, who was still lying down, was far away enough to only feel the shock waves but near enough to raise up and see his friend's bloody body lying on the ground with his arms and legs wreathing about in the air. Josef knew that his good friend was done for.

Within a few moments, Dieter's writhing stopped and he lay still and silent on the damp soil of Galicia. He had had no chance of survival. The blast from such close quarters had simply torn him apart. The others crowded around his limp bloodied body shocked and horrified by what had taken place. His once handsome face was not there anymore and his brain showed through his scull which was split wide open and his teeth protruded from his un-naturally open mouth and shattered jaw. Josef looked away. He felt sick. He was grief-stricken for Dieter, and wondered once more whether any of the group would ever see Germany again?

They had no shovel to bury their dead comrade so after someone had removed his boots, they lay his bloody body in the lake and placed some rocks on top of it to hold it down. As they watched, the body sank out of sight. Josef muttered to himself. "God Bless you Dieter, my brave, foolish friend."

"No fish tonight then?" Someone commented dryly. No one answered. They all felt too sick with shock. Everything had happened so quickly and the group were overwhelmed with grief for their lost comrade.

Josef knew that Dieter had a family in Munich before the war. That's what he was going home for. Dieter had left a wife and three children who would now be teenagers, all now without a father.

Josef was distraught and his mind cried out for some peace.

As the group mourned their comrade, Josef reminisced. Dieter had served with him from the early days, and Josef had considered him a special friend from the very beginning. He remembered that while in the Leningrad area where their unit had arrived in January 1942, Josef had been awarded an Iron Cross 2nd Class for helping his friend.

He remembered it well. His unit was south of Lake Ladoga when the Soviets were trying to break the siege of Leningrad. Josef's unit was by the Wolchow River when Dieter was hit in the leg and fell onto the hard snow in an exposed position in front of their dug out. Josef, perhaps foolishly, but without thought for himself, had run out from his cover to pull his friend back to the safety of their position. He knew that this was a dangerous thing to do under so much fire, but Dieter was his friend and good friends are special and rare. In his unit, it was accepted that they all looked out for each other and that applied to all the soldiers around him. None of them wanted to be there. They were all conscripts, and they just wanted the whole unit to survive the war and get home safely. Dieter had survived the ordeal and knew that he owed his life to Josef.

Josef wore his medal and ribbon with some pride, mounted through the second buttonhole down on his tunic, as was the custom. It wasn't so much the award he was proud of, but the fact that he had been able to save his comrade. That year, Josef had also been awarded the Winter Campaign Medal and an Infantry Assault Badge for his close hand to hand fighting.

He remembered another time while in Russia that a team from the propaganda ministry had come to his unit to make a newsreel. His unit had been warned to look clean, keen and happy as they took on an imaginary enemy ahead of them in order to show the people back home what a pleasure and honour it was to be fighting for the Fuehrer. The ministry must have been happy that day, as the battalion did not disappoint. They all feigned heroism and commitment as well as a little bravery. After the crew from the ministry finally departed, Josef's unit had, to a man, all laughed at what had just taken place.

"They will love it back home," said one.

"They don't know the half of it, do they?" said another. Josef remembered that they all had had too many beers to drink that night.

Now Josef's friend, Dieter was no more, and the group just wanted to put distance between themselves and the horrible tragedy. Josef was still limping and on roughly constructed wooden crutches, willing himself to go on. They walked for several more miles that day until the sun, set behind the pines ahead of them, when they found an old deserted barn. This was where they would stay that night.

Many of the timbers in the barn had rotted and fallen off. The weather was more damp than cold but there was the bonus of lots of straw to lie on which made it a good overnight place to rest. It was a place to forget or maybe to remember. After one of them made a small fire by rubbing dry sticks together, the group huddled together and were soon asleep.

Josef woke many times during that night. He couldn't get Dieter out of his mind. After so long a prisoner, it was terrible that his life had ended so quickly and tragically. He thought of the dead man's family in Munich. He remembered Dieter's views on the war and the National Socialists, which were similar to his own. Dieter had been a teacher before his call up, but that didn't save him. He had thought of leaving the country, but where would a German family go once the war had started? It had been impossible so he had to leave his wife and family, like Josef, and obey his orders. He had told Josef that he didn't know anyone in the unit who wanted to fight for the National Socialists but if you refused or complained you were sent to Dachau concentration camp for 'retraining,' and the name of that place put the fear of God into all soldiers.

Josef remembered all that footage he had seen over the years put out by the Ministry of Propaganda under Josef Goebbels. It always portrayed the German military as enthusiastic soldiers fighting for the Reich. They were conquering heroes, the master race always moving forward with a smile on their faces, serving their Fuehrer. That might have been the case for Dr Goebbels and his newsreels, but it wasn't the truth as he had seen it.

He had seen a hard, filthy, cruel, pointless war. The German army had aggressively gobbled up smaller nations and grabbed what they could for the Reich. Cruelty, needless killing of prisoners, both soldiers and civilians alike, for no real reason, had been endemic, and Josef wanted no part in it. He hated war; he hated the Nazis for ruining his country and his life. What he couldn't understand was how a country as cultured as Germany could also be so cruel. Yet, he knew that he was just a helpless pawn in the overall picture and could change nothing save perhaps his soul and his conscience.

He also recalled a pleasant experience in a charabanc in his early teens organised by the local church. It was to Eisenach, Thuringia, some three hours away from Sparneck. Just outside the town was the majestic castle of the Wartburg. Their guide had explained that Martin Luther had stayed in the castle in the 1520s following his ex-communication from the Catholic Church. It was there that he had translated the New Testament from old Greek into German.

The guide had also told them of the Wagner opera, Tannhäuser, set in the castle. It was in the Troubadour's Hall in the castle in the 13th Century that a singing contest had taken place. Wagner had made this contest famous in his opera. It had fascinated Josef who had closed his eyes and listened to the beautiful Overture being played on a record. He was overcome with emotion as he heard the beautiful music. The whole day had been a great success. It was the first time Josef had been any distance away from home, and it had made such a great impression on him that he had never forgotten it. What Josef couldn't understand was how a country so cultured as Germany could also be so cruel.

He understood for the first time that he was not only a Bavarian but also a German and outside his cosy home and village was a great country uneasy with itself and trying to come to terms with the Treaty of Versailles that had been imposed on it in 1919. His teacher spoke of nothing else. But he was a farmer's son, and after a few days, although the trip had affected him greatly, there were much more important things to think about, like the well-being of the cattle and where his parents would find their next meal.

Chapter Five - Goodbye Hans

In what seemed no time at all it was dawn, and Josef remembered that he had dreamt about the retreat from Russia in 1944. The German army had what was known as a scorched earth policy. As they retreated, or, as they called it, tactically withdrew, they burned and blew up everything that could have been of use to the enemy. The whole countryside seemed to be burning, as fields of wheat were set alight, bridges were blown, and rail lines ripped up. After the houses had been ransacked for food and weapons, they too were destroyed. The German army was leaving Russia in ruins in order to slow the advance of the Soviet army.

Josef's mind abruptly returned to the present, as the others called him to get ready. The cool, damp morning promised a fine day as Josef stretched, jumped up and down, relieved himself, and set off with the others on the road west.

The countryside was heavily wooded with coniferous trees on both sides of the road, casting it into deep shade for much of the day. Josef spotted deer occasionally dashing from side to side through the brush and sometimes a fox, but no cars, trucks or people were using the road. He thought it was strange that it was so quiet, just a few ex-German prisoners making their way home after years of confinement. He took a deep breath – he smelt freedom.

The group walked till midday, then took a break on the grass by the side of the road. One of the group, Christian from Bonn, went off a few paces to relieve himself. When he returned, he was carrying a long rusted iron bar that he said he believed had been used for holding barbed wire in place. It was about 1.5 metres long and at one end the iron was curled round a number of times like a spring. Christian swung it around his head saying, "I have a good idea for this piece of iron that might make us a dinner this evening."

After their short break, they carried on walking; chatting about what they would do when they got home and how good life would be in the future. Suddenly they saw a group of startled deer dart across the road just a few metres ahead of them. The group were as shocked as the deer to meet on that road. Christian sprinted ahead and threw his iron rod into the group. A young deer that had not been able to keep up with the others was hit. It fell to the ground with its limbs twitching. Christian ran up to it, picked up the iron rod, and gave it a coup de grace to the head.

The others caught up and congratulated Christian, who dragged the deer off the road to the edge of the forest. There, one of the group produced a small knife, and the still warm, twitching deer was cut up, while the others collected wood.

A couple of the group got the fire started by rubbing sticks together, and it wasn't long before the deer was being cooked, as the group waited eagerly licking their lips. When the meat was finally ready, they all enjoyed a fine meal. After they finished, and with full bellies, they all agreed that it was the best venison, in fact the best meal, any of them had ever tasted. Josef added dryly, "It's the only real meal we have had in years!" They all laughed, and pronounced Christian hero of the day.

After their nourishing meal, they continued walking for another two hours until they came to a concrete hut where they decided to spend the night. No one realized that it was by a railway line and a number of night trains would wake them up each time one thundered by. However, there was a place for a little fire in the hut, which, after a lot of trouble, they managed to light as the night was cold.

Warm and relaxed and still with full bellies, they all chatted and told jokes till the last of the men fell asleep. As Josef slept, he dreamt of President Hindenburg, the burly old man who had been Germany's president from 1925 till 1934 when he died, allowing Hitler and the Nazis to take power. Although a Prussian, Hindenburg had been Josef's father's hero of the 1st World War. It was Hindenburg and the German Army who had wiped the Russians off the map at the Battle of Tannenberg in East Prussia in August 1914. It had been a great battle and Josef's father had often spoken of it with great pride.

His father was so proud of that battle, but after the victories, there had come the defeats. Finally the war was lost and the Germans had to sign an armistice in a lounge car in the Forest of Compiegne in France. Germany lost 10% of its territory, and the Kaiser had abdicated and gone into exile in Holland. Times became really hard in Germany. There was massive inflation and huge unemployment. Josef's family had great difficulty surviving during those awful post war years, and they often went hungry.

The Compiegne Forest lounge car was used again in June 1940 when the French signed an armistice with Germany ending the Battle of France. Hitler chose the site due to its symbolic role as the site of the 1918 armistice. Germany had been avenged.

The group awoke not long after dawn, as none of them had slept too well. They decided that they wouldn't sleep near a railway line again unless it was absolutely necessary. Although it was early, and the sky was blue, the day was cool and damp. They walked all morning until the sun was high in the sky when they stopped again and ate the remainder of the deer they had killed the day before. There was just enough for all. After they finished they sat awhile dozing, before continuing their journey.

It was late afternoon and after walking for about three hours they saw off to their right a clearing with a farm not far away. Hopefully they might find some food and spend the night. It looked very peaceful with the cows quietly munching grass in a field in front of the farmhouse. The scene reminded Josef of when he was young. He was about six or seven. His father had told him that it was time he helped with the calving that was imminent. Josef had been excited at the prospect, which he saw as being grown up.

But when the time came, his excitement had turned to nausea as he watched the calve slipping gently out from its mother. He observed how the mother tenderly licked their young, which seemed so affectionate to him. He didn't realise the feeling and instinct a cow had for its young, it was rather like his mother's love for him.

Even at that early age, he was upset to learn that normally only the females survived, while the males were killed soon after birth for their meat. None of the new borns, either male or female, were allowed to remain more than two hours with their mothers. Josef remembered running from the cow shed crying as he heard the cows bellowing in grief as their young were taken from them. The whole episode had soured him from dairy farming. In later years when his father had died, he had cut back drastically on the dairy side of the farm and moved more into agriculture: wheat, barley and potatoes. He simply could not come to terms with what he felt was the cruelty of dairy farming.

As the group approached the farm, the peasants working in the field withdrew to the safety of the farmhouse. Josef realised that the ragged group of men approaching must have looked really threatening.

The leader of Josef's group, who spoke a few words of Polish, asked for some food. The farmer, probably more out of fear than generosity, said that he would see what he could find. The group made themselves comfortable in the farmyard and waited. Josef began to whistle the wartime song, "Lilly Marlene," and the others soon joined in with the words. Here were a group of German ex-prisoners in a Polish farmyard singing for their supper supplied by Polish peasants. Josef smiled.

About an hour elapsed before the farmer came back with black bread and sausage meat, served by his three voluptuous daughters. Quite hungry by now, the men ate very quickly. The farm seemed a good place to spend the night, so with the farmer's permission, they found a barn attached to the farmhouse where they could relax. The farmer requested that they did not smoke. Since none of them had even seen a cigarette in years, they readily agreed.

Once settled in the barn, Josef looked through his meagre possessions: the piece of Russian coal, his chess set, each piece skilfully crafted over several months from wood collected during the days when he marched back from the mine, and the little carving of the Madonna and Child. He was pleased that he had something to take home with him. He didn't know whether it was for him to remember his imprisonment or to try to forget it. But would he ever forget his years of captivity? Only time would tell.

After resting in the barn for a while, Josef became restless. It was a nice evening and still light, so he decided to take a walk outside before he turned in. He wanted to be on his own. He liked his own company; it gave him time to think, time to remember.

As he slowly walked, he remembered the times in Sparneck before the war. His thoughts turned to courting his darling Helma, their marriage, the birth of their beautiful son Siegfried, moving in with his parents in the family farmhouse, and learning from his father the skills of a farmer. His mother cooked and looked after his father. She was a wonderful "Hausfrau" and even though they were poor, she was proud of her home and family. When Helma moved in, she was of the same mould as his mother, and kept their part of the house spotless. She was a wonderful wife and mother and gave him great pleasure. Things were settled, and they all worked very hard on the farm to make a living. Those days were like one long summer. They had been halcyon days, a time of calm before the catastrophic storm that was to engulf them all.

After a little while of walking in the woods, he became aware of voices: Polish and German voices. He approached slowly, staying out of sight. What he saw shocked, amazed and interested him. At just a few meters in front of him between the greenery was one of his group, Hans Bauer, a young Berliner. He was rolling on the grass, his ragged trousers around his ankles, his white backside moving up and down. Josef put one hand over his mouth in order to stifle a laugh. Underneath Hans was one of the farmer's daughters. She had served the food earlier. Now she was half naked romping with his comrade, obviously serving him his desserts, Josef mused.

All three of the farmer's daughters had been keen to see so many men arrive at the farm. This one was the least handsome, somewhat heavy and big breasted, she looked quite a handful when stripped down to her underwear, which was in disarray around her flabby legs.

He watched as Hans gave this massive mare all he had, and he heard her sighs of pleasure as they had beautiful sex together. Josef kept his hand over his mouth in case he should make any noise, and just watched. It had been many years since he had made love to a woman and he felt quite envious of Hans now in the act However he consoled himself with the thought that he would have been hard pushed to have taken this wench in hand even after so many years.

At precisely the same moment, they both let out muted yells of relief as they finished their pleasure together. Hans kissed her in grateful thanks on the lips and she kissed him back. Then she quickly pulled back as though ashamed at what she had just done. As they stood up together, Hans adjusted his clothes and she wiped herself on her dress. Then curiously, Josef thought, she quickly ran off with her bloomers still in her hands. He thought this a very strange reaction to their lovemaking.

After his free peep show experience, Josef made his way slowly back to the farm following the stream. It was still warm and he felt quite relaxed as he meandered along kicking the dead leaves beneath his feet. On his way, he identified many species of plants that also grew in northern Bavaria.

When he arrived at the farm some little time later, it seemed as though all hell had broken out. Everyone was running around screaming. The farmer was jumping up and down with his hands in the air. "What's going on?" Josef asked one of his comrades?

"One of the farmer's daughter's is accusing one of us of raping her."

"What?" said Josef, "I just saw one of the girls with Hans in the woods together. It certainly wasn't rape. They were both enjoying the experience. Come to think of it, so was I!" he said with a grin on his face.

Everyone waited nervously in the farmyard for things to progress as the Poles screamed, cried, shouted and shook their fists in the air. Unknown to the group, the farmer had sent for the police and within a short time they arrived on the scene in a jeep with Russian markings.

The police looked at the rough gang in the farmer's yard and ordered them to stand in line to be identified. It crossed Josef's mind that perhaps they would all now be shot by the heavily armed police.

They all lined up and after a while, the daughter who had been with Hans, crying loudly and leaning heavily on her father's arm, with her hair and clothing in disarray, came out to identify her assailant. Josef thought it incredible that an hour or so earlier, she had been rolling around semi naked on the ground making love. She seemed to have had a change of mind, and her lovemaking had now become rape. More than likely, she was consumed with guilt at what she had done and what might be the outcome of her actions. She would have made a good actress, Josef thought.

The daughter walked, sullen -faced down the line of Germans, head bent forward, having supposedly been shamed and abused by one of these brutes. The aggrieved virgin glanced momentarily at each face until she came to Hans. She pointed towards him and began to shout and cry out loud. Hans just stood there trembling with fear, trying to explain in German that she had been an eager participant. Only the Germans knew what he was saying. No one else understood or cared. Here was an itinerant young German taking advantage of a Polish maiden. It was clear-cut! Someone had to be punished. The virgin had to be avenged. She had had her fun and now she wanted her revenge.

Hans screamed out for help from the others as he was pulled out of line. The policemen put their hands under his armpits, lifted him up, and pulled him along. His feet were dragging alone behind him as he screamed. They dragged him in the direction from which Josef had so recently returned, and where the pair had made love, or rather had sex!

"What are they going to do to him?" one of the group asked. A moment later, while they were still standing in line, they heard a single gun shot ring out and realised it was all over for Hans the Berliner. Only Josef knew the truth, but he stayed silent. There was no one to tell. There was no one who would have listened. There was no one who understood much German anyway. The Berliner had paid the ultimate price for the ultimate act. Hans the Berliner had been a fool.

He knew that Hans had, like him, been captured in the Battle of Berlin and remembered how they had both survived the years of incarceration in the Soviet Union. To die now for nothing, as that is what he had done, was senseless. It was yet another tragedy to befall the group.

When the police returned to the farmyard one, who spoke a few words of German, instructed them to take care of the filthy German rapist. They all fell out of line and went to the barn to collect spades to bury their dead comrade.

They walked slowly to the scene of the execution where they found Hans lying face down on the grass. He had fallen forward from his kneeling position, having been shot at point blank range in the back of the neck. His hands were tired behind his back. They cut the rope that restrained his wrists, turned him over and saw that his mouth and eyes were wide open in an expression of terror.

"He looks as if he is screaming," someone commented.

It was all over for Hans. Hopefully, he was now in some sort of peace. Someone closed his eyes and mouth then slowly the burial party dug a grave in the sandy Polish soil. Before they laid him in his final resting place, they went through the ritual of removing usable clothing from his limp body. Josef had his boots, another of the men his trousers, and someone else his shirt. Perhaps some would think they had desecrated the still warm body, but their needs were now greater than his. His only need was to rest in peace. For Hans the Berliner, the war was finally and tragically over. He lay in an unmarked grave with no stone or cross to mark where this once brave soldier had been buried.

None of the group wanted to linger at the farmhouse where the execution had taken place, so they left the farm at once and headed off into the dark. They spent that night some miles further on in a little fisherman's hut by a small lake. Josef was stunned, still in shock. He couldn't get the Berliner out of his mind: his soft voice, shy nature, and his youthful good looks. Josef knew he had to move on in his mind. He had seen so many horrors over the last sixteen years, and there was no point in dwelling on any of them. He realised that his war was not yet over and couldn't be until he reached home – if he ever did!

Chapter Six - Chased by a Mob

After another bad night's sleep, Josef opened his eyes and just lay there watching the sunrise and listening to the birds. He felt tired, but he was relaxed and it was already warm. He was still having difficulty getting Hans off his mind. After awhile his thoughts strangely turned to the day America declared war on Germany.

It was December 11th 1941, and the Japanese had attacked the US fleet at Pearl Harbour in Hawaii without a declaration of war. How this might affect him and the German Army he had no idea, but what he did know was that the Americans had retaliated by declaring war on Japan as well as the other axis countries, which included Germany. That had worried him at first as he was fighting in Russia at the time and thought that soon Germany might be fighting on two fronts. This would not be good for the National Socialists but maybe it could change the course of the war and he might get home sooner. Thoughts of getting home dominated his mind all the time, so anything that might end the war sooner seemed a positive development to him.

He was disturbed from his reverie by the others in the group calling out to him to get up and get ready to leave. He moved slowly at first, but finally did manage to get himself together. He picked up his little bundle of treasures and, in a short time, the group was ready to move on. They were quiet and reflective and all still in shock about losing Hans.

Turning their backs on the sun, they continued their long journey home. After a couple of hours in brilliant sunshine with the temperature rising all the time, they came to a Y junction. The road to the right showed Warsaw, which would take them in a northwesterly direction. The road to the left, a narrower road full of pot holes in which grass was growing, led in a more southwesterly direction and was sign-posted Krakow and Wrocslaw.

The general opinion was to go to the right, to Warsaw, where there might be transport heading west. They might be able hitch a ride to the border and beyond. Josef thought about it for a long while then chose to go left as his home was in the south of Germany, and he knew that Warsaw was in the north like Berlin. He had not heard of Wroclaw, but he knew of Krakow and knew that it was in southern Poland. In fact, he had learned at school that it had only been given to Poland at the end of the 1st World War. Before that, it had been in the province of Galicia in the Austro Hungarian Empire. So he thought that when he arrived there everyone might speak German.

As he thought about his decision a bit longer, he remembered the agony of crossing the Polish border alone and being detained. Should he stay with the rest of the group? It was a hard decision. In the end, he decided to head south on his own.

He said goodbye to his friends with whom he had shared so much, the indignities of prison life, the positive times of hoping one day to be free, and now this recent journey that brought them together sharing a common cause. They had become close and Josef was loath to leave them, but his mind was made up.

It was already late morning when he left the others with cheery goodbyes all round, and made off in the direction of Krakow and the mysterious city of Wroclav. It was a beautiful day with not a cloud in the sky, and he whistled as he walked to keep himself company. After some hours, he came to a small village called Debno where he thought he might get some food and drink.

He went straight to the town's pretty little square and sat down at a table in front of a local cafe. It was warm and quiet, and he enjoyed the peace. Shortly a large gentleman, the waiter, dressed in an off-white apron appeared from inside the building and asked what he would like. At least that's what Josef presumed he said.

"Drink," he said making the familiar movement of his hand to his mouth. The waiter nodded his understanding of the request and disappeared.

Josef sat there for sometime waiting to be served. He was just thinking how deserted the village looked, when suddenly he saw two men enter the other side of the square opposite from where he was sitting. Two others came out from a nearby shop and more appeared as if from nowhere. He began to panic a bit as he waited to be served, watching so many people so quickly entering the square. They moved unusually slowly around the perimeter of the square heading in his direction.

Suddenly and without warning, they charged towards him shouting "Germanski!" They began throwing stones at him, and their eyes burned with hate. There were at least a dozen of them, and Josef decided to make a quick retreat. He jumped up and ran through the bar, pushing aside the waiter who stood in his way, and disappeared out the back door into the yard. Jumping over a wooden fence, he ran out of the village with the angry mob in close pursuit continuing to throw stones and rubbish at him and shouting obscenities.

He was surprised at his own agility, as he was soon way ahead of them. He ran across a field of young barley and up a hill where he saw a cemetery, which he entered to hide from the pursuing mob. There he saw a group of mourners standing around an open grave. He joined the group and was soon lost in their number. He saw from the corner of his eye the mob that had been pursuing him pass by the cemetery disappearing into a wood beyond.

He realised now that he must be very cautious with the local population who seemed suspicious, aggressive and unfriendly towards him. If this were what some of the Poles were like he thought, then it wasn't safe for him to be around.

He stood panting as he listened to the padre speak with a sad voice. He couldn't understand a word of what was being said, but he could listen to the peaceful, deep voice, which somehow had a calming effect on him and the other mourners. He looked around those gathered and saw an elderly woman who he thought to be the widow. She was dressed in black and crying as she held a white handkerchief to her eyes. After watching her for a while, Josef became aware that she looked very much like his own mother or how she had looked when Josef was young.

He kept looking at her and wished that his own mother were still alive. He admired her silver-grey curly hair, her deeply furrowed skin, her long thin fingers, and felt a lump in his throat. Suddenly she looked up and their eyes met.

"Jan," she said out loud, her face turning from one of sorrow to one of joy. Josef was surprised that she seemed to recognise him. She edged towards him and gently put an arm around him resting the side of her face on his chest.

"Jan," she said again and then said something in Polish that was lost to him. He looked down and smiled at her, and she smiled back. It really was like being with his own mother again.

Why these Poles should be friendlier to him than the others who had so recently chased him he did not know. The widow and Josef stood together holding hands until the padre had finished speaking, and the grave was being filled in. Josef then turned to the mourners and asked if anyone present could speak German and received a number of replies.

One of the mourners told him that the burial was for the widow's husband who had died recently. She now thought that Josef looked like her son who had been killed in the war. Josef replied that strangely he felt the same familiarity with her, and that she looked similar to his mother who had passed away many years earlier.

"Please tell her she reminds me of my own mother," he said. As one of the crowd told the widow what Josef had said, the others all thought that this was very strange but if it cheered the widow, then it would be ok. Josef watched her face, which turned into a large smile. She hugged him again burying the side of her face on his chest. Then she said the word "syn."

"It means son," added someone in the crowd. "You are lucky. She thinks you look like her son."

The widow said something to the padre and with Josef's arm tucked under hers the pair turned and walked out of the cemetery together.

It was a short way back to the widow's house on the edge of the village, and near where he had so recently been forced to leave in such a hurry. When they arrived at her front door, she stooped, fumbling for her key, which took her some time to find. When she opened the door, she pushed Josef in first, babbling all the time, although he could not understand a word she said.

She indicated that he should sit down, and after taking off her coat, she went to the kitchen to prepare a meal. The radio was turned on, and Josef fell asleep dreaming of being chased by the mob. He wondered what would have happened to him had they caught him? He thought probably a bloody stoning and imagined himself lying on the ground being kicked and bludgeoned by the angry group.

It was already dark when she woke him with a kiss on his forehead, and spoke something comforting. The only word he caught was "syn." She dished up the dinner, which was delicious. He feasted on dumplings in goulash very similar to what his own mother would have made him all those years ago.

After a number of vodkas, which she served one after another, she stood up and beckoned him to follow her. She showed him to a room with a large bed in it and wished him goodnight. That seemed to be the same in both their languages. Josef slept well that night and dreamed of home.

Early next morning he was awakened with a cup of hot chocolate and some sweet biscuits. He looked for his clothes but they were nowhere to be found. He asked in sign language where his clothes were. With a smiling face, she pointed out of the window where he saw his clothes hanging on the clothesline. She indicated that he should wear a dressing gown, which was folded, neatly and hanging over a chair.

After he had put this on, she took him into the kitchen where he saw a tin bath full of hot water and she pointed to him. He thanked her and waited until she had left the room before he stripped off his dressing gown and pants and got into the bath that was so small that he had to bend his legs to sit down.

He sat there rather uncomfortably but grateful for the bath as he thought about what to do next. Shortly, the widow re-entered the room and indicated that she was going to wash his back. He was very embarrassed but did as he was told. She scrubbed his back with a bar of cold soap, then said a few words, and left the room. When he had finished bathing he got out of the bath, dried himself and put the dressing gown back on.

Returning to the snug little parlour, he found, to his surprise, a table laden with all sorts of food. He hadn't seen so much food on a table since his childhood, and then only at Christmas. The widow poured coffee and he ate and drank until he was full. It was the best breakfast in years and he thanked her very much.

He spent the rest of the morning in an outside shed repairing the boots that he had so recently acquired from Hans. There seemed to be everything a handyman could need in the work shed. Josef had felt uncomfortable wearing Han's boots, not only because they needed repair, but also because he had been taught never to wear dead man's boots. In this case, however, he thought his need was greater than his fear of the old saying.

Lunch was similar to breakfast but included a bowl of soup first. When he had finished lunch, the widow led him back to the bedroom where she pointed to his clean, freshly pressed clothes that were lying at the end of the bed.

Josef looked at this frail little figure, bowed, and said thank you. She understood and gave him a big hug and a kiss on his forehead. In the afternoon, he cleaned her windows and chopped wood for her large oven that, although situated in the parlour, would have heated the whole house in the cold weather.

Although it was now nearly summer, and the oven was not in use, he knew that the amount of wood he had cut for her would last a long time when winter finally came round again, and she needed the oven for cooking and heating.

After doing all the chores, he would have liked to take a stroll outside but was fearful that the mob may see him and finish their dirty work. He began to ponder how he was ever going to leave this lovely old lady without breaking her heart and upsetting himself. Yet he knew that he had to go; he had to get home.

That night, after she had seen him to bed with a drink of hot chocolate and a kiss on his forehead, he waited a short time before he quietly got up and dressed. He could hear her snoring softly and evenly in her little bedroom, so he knew she was asleep. He went into the garden and picked a handful of beautiful late spring flowers, which he took back into the house. He put the flowers in an empty vase and quietly filled it with water. He then turned and left the house. "Goodbye, Mother," he whispered as he silently closed the door.

It had been quite a strange experience meeting this widow. It seemed so surreal. He would never be able to explain for the rest of his life how there was such an affinity between the two of them. They had both felt this, and now he was probably going to break her heart. She would feel as if she were losing her son for a second time.

Chapter Seven - No Absolution

Josef found the main road again, pleased that it was densely forested on both sides. The tall pines seemed at the same time both beautiful and threatening, but it was also a place where he could quickly take cover if need be. There was an almost full moon giving a silvery sheen to the road, that Josef saw stretched straight ahead for miles.

After he had walked for about an hour, he decided it would be a good place to spend the rest of the night so he found a little spot off the road where he could see through the trees in both directions. He felt he would be well hidden in the deep undergrowth, as he curled up there and fell asleep.

When he woke up, it was already light. He knew that he had only slept for a couple of hours, but he felt fine. He set off once more along the road that remained heavily forested. He thought it curious that, although a major road, there was little traffic. In fact, it occurred to him that he was seeing more wildlife than traffic.

He hadn't been walking for too long when he heard the sound of gunfire ahead of him. Just a single shot from a rifle at first, then another shot and another. He was curious to know where the gunfire was coming from. When he got closer to the sound of the gun shots, he left the road and entered the forest. He noticed an old bike leaning against a tree, as another shot rang out close by. He went further into the forest when he suddenly heard a voice in Polish call out to him. Josef looked up and there he saw a figure dressed in green, wearing a grey felt hat with a large feather in it. He was holding a rifle and was high up in the dense foliage on a wooden hunter's lookout platform.

Josef called out to him, "Hallo, I am Josef Holz from Germany. I am on my way home to Bavaria." A few moments elapsed before he heard a rifle being cocked and another shot rang out. Josef realised this time that the shot was meant for him. He dodged behind a tree out of the hunter's line of fire.

"I am on my way home to Bavaria," he repeated. "I have been a prisoner of the Russians for many years, and now just want to go home."

There was another shot aimed in his general direction, but this too, like the last one, went wide. Josef froze! He stood totally still and silent as he heard the hunter reloading his rifle. Then came a volley of fire that ricocheted around him, but thankfully none found their intended target.

As he stood motionless and silent behind the tree, he heard the sound of sticks cracking as the hunter climbed down out of the tree and began looking in the undergrowth for the body he thought he had just hit. Josef remained quiet behind the tree as the hunter came closer. He was in his late fifties, a bear of a man with a grey beard and a red, deeply scared face. The scar on the left side of his face dragged his eye down, exposing the red of his inner eye, making him look grotesque. Without a sound, Josef turned slowly and picked up a large, thick cosh-like piece of wood that lay beside him on the ground.

As the hunter came level with the tree where Josef was hiding, Josef jumped out at him swinging his club and knocking the rifle out of the hunter's hand.

The hunter's face contorted with hate as he screamed "Germanski! Germanski!" and lunged at Josef.

Josef took the full force of the giant's body and fell backwards onto the damp soil with his assailant on top of him punching, spitting and screaming. At first Josef thought he had the upper hand, being the younger and more agile. However, he soon realised his aggressor was the stronger, as they rolled over and over in the deep undergrowth punching and tearing at each other.

Josef knew he would need all his strength to overpower his adversary. He was tiring and losing his strength, as he lay under this giant of a man. The Pole growled and spat in Josef's face. Josef felt consumed with hatred for this man he didn't even know, who was trying to kill him, and stop him, from getting home.

Grabbing the piece of wood he had found earlier, he smashed it into the Pole's face. The hunter screamed out in pain as he fell backward. This gave Josef the advantage, and he leapt on top of the Pole. Time and time again Josef smashed at his face with the club. He heard the cracking of his scull and saw the blood spurting out from his eye sockets, as Josef pulverized the Pole's face with the heavy piece of wood.

From under him, Josef heard another loud scream of pain. It was the last scream the Pole would ever make as he lay there covered in blood, dead. Without thinking what he was doing, Josef continued smashing at the Pole's bloody face until he realised there was no longer any point. When he finally stopped and came to his senses, he was appalled at his own violence and screamed out a long, slow "No!" It was a cry for help that echoed through the forest. He looked down at what he had done and was shocked, horrified and disgusted. Not even during the darkest days of the war had he ever lost his temper like this. He had never killed a man in this way before.

Getting up, Josef looked at the bloody mess lying on a bed of dry leaves in front of him. He stood over the body for a few moments panting, trying to get his breath back. He said a prayer to be forgiven and to bless the soul of this dead man. It was like in the war all over again, killing someone he didn't even know.

Finally, he took the bloody corpse by the ankles pulling it deeper into the forest and away from the lookout platform. Placing the rifle beside the body, as he didn't want to be seen in the future carrying a firearm, he covered the hunter's last resting place with earth, dried leaves and sticks as best he could. He knew that the wolves, which were prevalent in packs in the area, would find the body long before any humans.

He moved the dead Pole's bike from the tree and laid it some distance from the body covering it with leaves. It occurred to him that he could have used the bike himself but he didn't want to be linked in any way with the crime. He considered the word "crime." It wasn't a crime; it was self-defence.

He turned and took one last look at the makeshift grave and felt remorse. He had killed this man, a total stranger, who was so full of hate for him only because he was a German. Maybe, like himself, the hunter had been a man full of memories, but the Pole, damaged by the war, had been unable to forgive, unable to forget. Now he was no more, lying under the leaves and dirt with his rifle by his side with his head caved in. Josef knelt down a little way from the corpse and whispered, "Dear Lord, may this be the last death of the Second World War." He stood up, brushed himself down and continued his journey for a few miles before stopping to rest at the edge of the forest as he waited for night to fall. Then he began to walk again.

He walked all night and luckily the weather was fine. The sky was clear and the stars shone brightly to help guide his way. When morning came, he found a comfortable place to sleep in the forest. There was a small stream nearby and before he made his bed under a tree on crisp dry leaves, he washed himself thoroughly. He didn't sleep well as he could not forget the hunter. The incident in the forest had upset him. He just wanted to get out of Poland, but he knew he had quite some way to go and without the company of his comrades, he felt vulnerable and exposed to attack and misfortune.

At dusk, he started walking again. A number of times he had to dodge back into the cover of the forest to hide as trucks drove by, but despite this, he managed to walk a long way that night. He wanted to get as far as possible from the scene of the incident. Occasionally he heard wolves howling in the distance. Were they howling for his blood or had the pack found the body of the hunter?

When daylight came, he found a little wayside shrine on the edge of a field. In this small shelter, he slept well and long. As he slept, he had a strange dream of the day he heard the news of the attempt on the life of Adolf Hitler on 20th July 1944 at Rastenburg in East Prussia. The would-be assassin, Count Claus von Stauffenburg, had placed a brief case containing a bomb under a table near to where Hitler was standing. The bomb went off but Hitler was not killed. Dreadful retribution followed for the conspirators and for those even suspected of knowing about the plot. Josef woke up with a start. He was sweating and fearful that he had known about the plot and was being hunted, but soon realised that it was only a dream.

In reality, Josef had been fighting a rearguard action in Russia at the time. After three years of victories, and always on the offensive, the tables had turned and the Germans were on the defensive and falling back. Josef secretly wished that the attempt on Hitler's life had been successful. There would have been a new German government and possibly the new leaders would have found a way to a peaceful ending of the war. He could have been home in the autumn of 1944 and would not have been a prisoner for ten long years in Russia. Why he had had the dream he didn't know. The mind plays strange tricks, he thought.

It was dark when he woke up in his little shrine. He stood up rather stiffly, stretched and began walking again   After only a short while, he saw houses with lights twinkling spread out ahead of him in the distance and realised he was heading toward a large town. As he drew nearer to the town, a bus swept by him from a side road. It had a sign displaying the word Krakow on the front. Josef was excited to be arriving in a place he had actually heard of. He finally felt he was getting nearer to his home. He made his way to the centre of the city where he crossed a bridge over the river and saw it was sign posted Vistula River.

As it was a warm night, he found a solitary park bench immediately and fell asleep. When he awoke, it was just getting light. He saw an old man sweeping the path nearby, and called out to him, "Krakow?"

"Da, Krakow," came the reply, somewhat aggressively. "Krakow, Polen."

Josef didn't know too much about Poland but saw in the sunlight what a beautiful city it was, and he knew too that it had been the capital of Poland during the war. He decided to climb Wawel Hill on which stood an ancient cathedral and castle. He wanted to pray, for deliverance from evil and ask, if it were the Lord's will, that he be allowed to get home safely to his family.

Josef was a Roman Catholic; most Bavarians were. He hadn't had much encouragement, time, or inclination for the Christian religion over the last years, but now, as he entered the beautiful cathedral, he was overcome with emotion. He dropped to his knees and felt warm tears running down his cheeks.

He looked through the rays of sun that shone through the high windows above the alter and began to pray: "Lord, have you forgotten me?" That was how he felt, that his Lord had forgotten him, pushed him aside, given him up as lost. "If you have, dear Lord," he continued, "please don't give up on my family. Please bless my dear wife Helma and my boys Siegfried and Herman and may they stay safe in your love, waiting for my return."

"Where are they then?" said a voice quietly in German. It was a priest and Josef realised that he had been praying out loud and been overheard. Even whispers travel far in a cathedral! Josef apologised and told the priest that his family were in Bavaria and he hadn't seen them for many years. He explained he had been a war prisoner of the Russians since 1945. The priest understood good German and Josef continued.

"Father?" he asked. "It has been many years since my last confession. Will you listen to it now?" The priest agreed to Josef's request and they entered the confessional box.

Josef opened his heart to the priest although he omitted the episode with the hunter. Tears ran down Josef's cheeks as the priest listened in silence. When he had finished, he sat back and waited for the priest to speak.

"Son, and you are my son, I cannot give you absolution for your sins. They must remain with you for the rest of your life and in the hereafter. You fought for the most evil regime ever, and I will not help you to atone for your sins. I will pray for your soul; that's all I am prepared to do. Now please leave the cathedral!"

Josef protested to the priest that he had been conscripted into the army, that he never wanted to go, and that he was never a member of the Nazi party. He hated the Nazis who had ruined his life and the lives of millions of others.

"Father, I was," he corrected himself, "I am, just a simple farmer from Bavaria."

The priest stood up and left the confessional without even looking back at Josef or wishing him God speed. Josef angrily called after him, "Thank you, Father, for your help and understanding and your Christian charity, and your forgiveness." He raised his voice shouting loudly as the priest disappeared into the vestry with Josef's voice resounding throughout the cathedral.

Josef's head was reeling as he sat down heavily on a pew in disbelief. After a short while, when he had recovered somewhat, he slowly stood up and left the cathedral. Where was the forgiveness the Church taught? He knew in his heart that he had always been an honourable soldier and to hear these words from the priest was deeply offensive and troubling to him. With that thought, he turned and left the cathedral. His own Church had wronged him, he knew it. He was angry and deeply hurt.

He walked back down the hill into the park where he had slept. It was a beautiful day and the park looked green and welcoming. All the people looked so happy. He saw some nuns eating their lunch from a large basket. It was a very tranquil scene and Josef felt he needed their company.

He hailed them and bid them God Bless. "God Bless you too, Brother," they called back in German. He was surprised to hear his mother tongue in this city, especially after so recently being harshly dismissed from the confessional by the Polish priest.

"Come join us," they bid him. "We have far too much food anyway."

He sat down on the warm grass beside them and shyly took a sandwich. "Thank you," he said. "Have more," they insisted. So he ate his fill of the beautiful, fresh sandwiches thinking they were the best he had ever tasted: rye bread, creamy butter, salami, cucumber and pâté.

When he finished, he told them his story. He told them that sometimes he thought he would never make it home and that he thought the Lord had forgotten him.

"God would never forget you," said one of the nuns rather sternly.

"With God's guidance and help, you will make it, Josef," said another, adding, "We will pray for you."

Josef asked why three German nuns were in Krakow, and they told him about the occupation that had lasted six long, bitter years. Now they, in co-operation with the German government, were trying to repair some of the damage done by assisting the Polish Catholic Church. They all agreed that this would be an uphill struggle.

"The Communist government here has no time for the Church," said one of the nuns.

"Many of the priests at the cathedral are really Communists you know."

"Yes, I do know," replied Josef. "I think I just met one!"

"God moves in mysterious ways his wonders to perform," replied a nun who until this point had remained silent. "But everyone will meet his maker one day to be judged," she added.

Josef replied, "And you are all wonders. Thank you for what you are doing here, and thank you for the wonderful meal you shared with me. God Bless you all." The nuns bid him farewell and wished him every success in getting home to Bavaria.

As he set off, he looked around at the lovely city that seemed to have survived the ravages of the war intact. He was glad to have passed through but was saddened by the attitude of the Church. Was he always to be labelled a sinner because of his war service? He was a farmer not a soldier, and he just wanted to get home. He walked faster as he left the city following the sign for Katowitz or as the sign showed, Katowice.

He walked for half a day passing some beautiful scenery. In the late afternoon, he found a derelict house by the side of the road and decided to take a nap. There he slept through the whole evening and night. When he finally woke, he realised that he had been asleep for a very long time. He decided he would now chance walking in the day again as he felt he was nearing home and perhaps it would be a little safer.

It was fine and dry as he set off. He could hear the bees humming as they collected pollen from the wild gorse that grew in profusion along the road. In the background, was the beautiful birdsong of hedge sparrows and blackbirds. The air was warm and Josef felt a surge of energy run through his body.

Later that morning, he came to the small town of Oswiecim. It seemed industrial and far from pretty, and he had already decided not to stop there. Shortly, he found himself walking past some red brick barracks. Over the large iron gates, which stood open, was a sign: Arbeit Macht Frei (Work Brings Freedom).

Josef instantly knew what this was. It was a concentration camp, but he had not previously heard of the name of Oswiecim. Just then he heard German voices and saw a group gathered around a guide. Josef walked up to the man and asked whether the place had a German name. The German-speaking guide looked at Josef and replied to his question.

"It was known as Auschwitz, Sir, and this was the main camp where the German guards were billeted who worked at the extermination camp of Birkenau which is just up the road. The soldiers lived well here. However, the inmates in the other camp barely survived. They were housed in large wooden huts where they stayed until they were murdered, sometimes only a short time after their arrival."

"So it was a prison camp then?" asked Josef.

"No Sir," said the guide, "It was an extermination camp run by the SS where a million Jews from all over Europe were brought to be killed by gas and then their bodies were burned and their ashes scattered. The killings went on till the Russians captured the camp on 27th January 1945. What they found appalled even them, and they were hardened fighters."

Josef was taken aback by what the stranger had said, unable to take in or believe what he had just heard. "No! I don't believe it!" he said out loud in total disbelief.

"If this were true then who did it? In whose name could such crimes be committed?"

"I suppose in the name of the German people," came the reply from the young guide.

"No," said Josef, "it was the Nazis"

The guide looked at him blankly, "is there a difference?"

"Of course," Josef came back somewhat annoyed that anyone would confuse the two.

"Of course there is," he repeated. "We all suffered under the Nazis, including the German people."

"We, I don't see the difference between the two," the guide said.

Josef knew he should not get into an argument with the guide, even if he did not agree with him.

"It was terrible for all of us, please believe me," Josef concluded.

Josef thought that Germany was a cultured nation, "The land of poets and thinkers."

He knew that there had been some awful barbarity on both sides during the war, in Russia by the Soviets and in Germany by the Gestapo and SS whom he knew were ruthless. But this? It seemed impossible.

He had heard rumours of mass killings but there were always rumours in war when everything seemed larger than life, and became exaggerated. He never really paid much attention to them. He was a Bavarian farmer conscripted into the German army. He was not political and he never felt that he was fighting for the National Socialists. He was fighting, he thought, for the wrongs done to Germany and because he had no choice. He would rather have stayed on his farm producing milk and barley. As it was, his main challenge had been just staying alive and surviving.

He stopped for a while and listened to people talking. The comments they made and the feelings they expressed toward the German people horrified him. He felt hated and shamed, so he decided to just keep walking. He could not, he would not, believe all the things he had heard that morning. Was it all a lie? It could be lies of the victors over the vanquished Germans. If it were the truth, it was unbelievable and unforgivable.

Josef continued west toward the city of Katowiec. What he had learned that day had disturbed him, and he felt greatly distressed that he should have been fighting on the side of the perpetrators of such crimes if what he had heard was true. He felt that if these things were true, all he had been through had been worthless and for nothing.

When he left Oswiecim, he never looked back. He wanted to forget the things he had been told even though he never would. It was already late in the day so he just kept walking.

Chapter Eight - Arrival in Breslau

Josef was glad to get out of the town of Auschwitz as he was totally shocked by what he had been told happened there. He still could not believe the things he had heard. Six million Jews murdered by the Nazis in the name of the German people and over a million of them in Auschwitz alone? It was not possible! How could people hate like that? How could civilized people do such things? He knew at least one Jewish family, the Goldsteins. They lived in Münchberg, a town near his farm, and ran the local butcher shop. They were the nicest of people. Josef wondered if they were still alive.

He passed through a number of small towns and villages until he came to Ledziny where he stopped just outside the town and took a short break. But he was restless and couldn't settle. Within a short time he was on the road again in the direction of Katowice. This was the town he knew as Katowitz that, before the war, had been a famous centre of German science, industry and culture.

When he arrived in the town he found it very depressing. Much of it was still in ruin and the buildings that were still standing, looked dilapidated and uncared for like many of the other towns he had passed through. The day was grey and the town accentuated this mood of gloom.

He wandered around hoping to find something to eat. Eventually, he came upon a stable and looked inside where he saw two horses. He knew a thing or two about horses and these looked half starved.

A voice called out to him in Polish. Josef replied "Germanski," and made the familiar hand to mouth sign he had used, with varying degrees of success, in the past.

The Pole indicated that if he wanted food, he would have to work for it. Josef agreed and cleaned the stable and groomed the poor, thin horses.

After a while, the Pole returned with salami and black bread on a wooden platter with a mug of beer. Josef finished the meal quickly and asked if there was any more.

"Niet," the Pole replied firmly. He then produced harnesses, which Josef fitted on the horses. Over his lifetime, Josef had owned many horses. They worked in his fields and moved heavy loads on his farm. He knew how to care for his horses. He also knew that these two horses were not cared for and looked very weak.

He was reminded of his two Alsatian dogs, Rolf and Helli who used to pull the carts around the farm laden with hay. They were beautiful dogs, very obedient and loving, although Josef remembered that Helli could be a bit snappy if she were overworked. He always seemed to be apologising for her to unhappy neighbours who had been bitten.

Following the Pole, Josef led the two horses into the yard and attached them to two carts, one stacked high with coal, which Josef was expected to drive, and the other with some logs. The Pole indicated that Josef should follow him in the cart.

"We go! We go!" he called out in German. Josef obeyed, as he was grateful for the breakfast the Pole had provided.

He could see that they were heading into town. Josef guessed that it was market day and the Pole hoped to make a bit of money selling his fuel. They set off at a slow pace towards the town centre, the horses heaving and snorting loudly as they laboured under their heavy loads. After a short while, as they neared town, Josef felt his horse lurch forward falling onto its front knees heavily with a loud grunt. Josef called out to stop, and the Pole turned around with an irritated look on his face and did as he was bid.

Josef knew the horse was done for and not even fit for the knacker's yard as it had no meat on it. The Pole dismounted, came back to Josef, looked at the horse and made a cutting motion with his hands across his neck. Josef knew what that meant. The horse was finished. With difficulty, they removed its harness and dragged the poor, limp creature to the side of the road.

A policeman was called and the Pole spoke to him. The policeman came over, drew his pistol from its holster that hung from his belt and shot the horse at point blank range. Josef drew back appalled at what he had seen. He had become inured to certain types of violence, but this made him feel sick. Although the horse would no longer have to suffer, this would not have had to happen if he had been properly cared for. Josef had seen enough. He decided to leave immediately, to get away from this depressing place.

He would make his way to Wroclav where he hoped he might find an indication of where the town of Breslau was. He called to the Pole that he was off and quickly left the grizzly scene. He heard the Pole calling out something behind him, but Josef did not look back.

Once he was out of the city, he walked for many hours until it was dark. He slept that night in a hut he discovered by the side of the road at the edge of the forest where he slept soundly. When he awoke next morning he could hear voices, and he realised it was a hut for railway workers who had just begun arriving for work. He left quickly before they could tell him to clear off. The railway line at that point followed the road and although he did not see many trains, those he did see were very old, dirty steam trains built long before the war.

Once back on the road, he hailed the first truck that came by. It was a tanker carrying milk. He asked for a lift, but when the driver realised Josef was German, he shouted at him and drove off.

A few minutes later he could hear another vehicle coming his way. It was a coal delivery truck. He hailed it and again asked for a lift. This time he was lucky. The driver was not unfriendly, but as they couldn't find a common language, they just smiled at each other from time to time. After a short ride, the truck stopped and the driver pointed up a side road indicating that he was turning off. Josef thanked the man and got out.

He walked until the late afternoon, when he happened to see a cyclist passing by. He pointed toward the town in the distance ahead of him, and called out, "Breslau?"

"Niet," the cyclist replied and without stopping called back over his shoulder, "Wroclaw; Breslau finish!"

"Finish?" Josef said out loud. If the cyclist were correct, Breslau, capital of the German region of Lower Silesia was now called Wroclaw in Poland. He reasoned that the Germans had lost the war so maybe they had also lost the territory. Now he understood why Katowitz had been spelt differently.

He hoped he were wrong. He couldn't visualise Germany without a large portion of the eastern territories, areas that included cities such as Marienbad, Katowitz, Gleiwitz Tichau, Tilsit and many others, all so overwhelmingly German towns. Surely they couldn't all now be in Poland? He wondered what had happened to the people?

He knew from his history lessons when he was a boy, that Silesia had been German for more than two hundred years. Fredrick the Great of Prussia had annexed it in 1742 at the Treaty of Berlin from Maria Theresa, the Austrian Hapsburg empress. Josef's geography hadn't been his best subject at school, but he knew there were a lot of German lands in the east. He also knew that Germany had lost Alsace Lorraine including the city of Strassburg after the First World War so maybe it was history repeating itself but this time in the east.

When he reached the city, he sat down on a bench in some pretty public gardens. Amazed, not knowing or understanding where he was, he felt as if he were in a bad dream. What he did know was that, wherever he was, he still had a long way to go. Then it began to rain.

He took cover in a shop doorway, but was soon told to clear off, so he moved on to a department store and was surprised at the lack of merchandise on offer. It was warm and he was wet. It was sale time and there were lots of people in there. In a little while, an official, dressed in a smart brown uniform with a hat that had a large red star above the peak, ordered him out of the store. Josef didn't understand a word the man said to him, but he knew what the red star meant! He also knew what the pointing finger to the door meant. Quickly, he left the store.

He wandered through the now almost deserted, wet city centre where there were still many buildings in ruin, until he came to the main square. There he sat down to take in the devastation of this once great city. After a while it stopped raining, and the sun came out to dry the damp streets.

By then he was feeling pangs of hunger, and decided to press on. He came to another bridge over the Oder River where he stopped in the middle, and once again drifted into thought. He liked his own company. He had become withdrawn over the years of his imprisonment and had learned it was always better to hold his tongue and keep his thoughts and opinions to himself. He had become self-sufficient and content with his own company even though he never stopped missing his wife and family.

He had been standing on the bridge for only a few minutes when he heard the sound of screeching brakes as a van pull up behind him. Suddenly, he heard running feet and then felt the point of a rifle in his back.

It was the police.   What had he done now, he thought?   Before he could answer his own question, he was bundled into the back of the vehicle which sped off in the direction from which he had so recently come.   Once inside the vehicle he had handcuffs fitted to his wrists and manacles to his ankles.   He was told to shut up even though he hadn't spoken a word.   He sat wondering what he would be accused of this time and whether he would ever get home.

The vehicle stopped with a shudder.   "Get out!" screamed a guard dressed in a dark green uniform. Josef obeyed the command.   He was very uncomfortable as the handcuffs were too tight and his manacled ankles only allowed him to shuffle. A feeling of great apprehension welled up inside him as he wondered whether the body of the old hunter had been discovered.

He was pushed from the vehicle into a small interview room in a drab building that smelt of damp and cigarettes and was as cold as ice.   The paint was peeling from the walls and there were watermarks on the ceiling.   His handcuffs and manacles were removed and he was ordered to strip.   Josef always felt uncomfortable about stripping although he had done so many times during his years of captivity.   Now he was doing it again.   When he had removed all his clothes, a massive woman dressed in a brown uniform appeared carrying a camera.   He was ordered to stand on a raised box and was slowly photographed from all angles.

"Arms above your head, arms behind your head, arms on your hips, arms outstretched, arms behind your back!" she shouted. When the photographer had finished, Josef was ordered off the stand and pushed into a little yard.

As he was shoved along, he lost his balance and fell as a strong cold stream of water was aimed at him. He cried out as he lay helpless on the wet, slippery cobbles. He tried to stand up, but the pressure of the icy water made it impossible, so he just lay there rolled up in a ball. His mind cried inside for his ordeal to end. Around him, a whole group of policemen and women stood by laughing, as they watched this wretched German turn and writhe in distress.

After a while, the water was switched off and he was ordered to get up off the floor. He was pushed back into the little room where his clothes were thrown back at him.

He looked at his clothes. They were just rags, and rags were all he possessed. They were the total sum of his life at this time, a few rags and his little bag of treasures.

Once he had put his clothes back on over his wet body, he was pushed down into a chair and told to wait for the chief examiner to arrive. Sometime later a greasy little man in uniform came in, sat down, and introduced himself as Ivan.

The chief examiner, who spoke good German, questioned Josef for some hours regarding a death in a forest to the east of the city.

"An old hunter was attacked and violently murdered," his interrogator said.

Josef's stomach turned over with fear. So the body had been found then, he thought. The chain-smoking interrogator blew smoke into Josef's face as he continued to fire question after question at him.

Josef repeatedly said that he could not answer the questions, as he didn't know anything. He said that he knew nothing about a hunter being killed. He was only a poor, hungry man trying to get back to his home after ten years a prisoner of the Russians.

"If you admit everything, you will save us all a lot of time and trouble. Admit and we can finish with this. In the meantime, the area of the crime is being searched for evidence to link you to this outrage."

Josef could not and would not admit to anything they were accusing him of doing. He realised that so far they had no evidence linking him with the crime, so he remained silent. He knew that what he had done was totally in self-defence, and that it was either himself or the hunter who had to die in that forest. He knew too that he would get no justice if he explained how the hunter came to die. He felt that his first concern was to his family, and to get home.

After more time and more questions, the interrogator roughly dragged Josef from the room and threw him into a cell with no bed, no running water and no toilet.

"Think about it, German. Think what I have told you. Admit now and we can shoot you in the morning, and it will be all over."

Josef's stomach turned over with fear in case some evidence were found linking him to the dead hunter. He spent an awful night in the cell and hardly slept at all. When he did, he dreamt of being led to a gallows, past lines of grinning faces jeering at him and screaming, "Die you German bastard, die in agony." Josef awoke suddenly in a sweat. He was still in the cold, damp, dark cell that stunk of urine, including his own. He could not settle and didn't sleep again that night. Pacing the cell, the hours passed very slowly.

In such low spirits, his mind also turned to Günther Kramer, who had been his best friend in the army. They had trained together, were both from Bavaria and were like brothers. They had been through all kinds of scrapes together and held each other in great respect.

Then came the day in 1944 when Günther had been badly wounded in the neck. With his arms across his chest, he had begged Josef to finish him off.

"I am done for Josef, my dear friend. Please end it now for me; please don't let me suffer. Help me to die like a soldier." Josef had looked into his friend's eyes and at the massive wound oozing blood from his neck. He could not bring himself to do what was asked of him.

Josef knew that if he left Günther, the advancing Russians would kill him, yet he still could not bring himself to kill his friend.

"Give me my gun, Josef," Günther implored.

Josef reluctantly did as he was asked. He took the gun from the leather holster that lay beside his friend, gave it to him, and looked away.

Josef heard the single shot ring out and looked around to see Günther's limp, bloody body. He was dead, a bullet hole through his temple. His suffering was over. Josef wept because he had lost his best friend and also because he had not been strong enough to help his comrade at the time of his greatest need. He promised himself then that when the war was over, if he survived the hell, he would visit Günther's wife in Augsburg and tell her about her husband's death: how brave he had been, and what good friends they had become.

Josef's mind returned to his present situation. He was in total despair and wished that he now had a gun to end his own agony.

Soon after it became light, he was once again brought roughly from the cell to the interrogation room where the officer asked if he had changed his mind.

"I cannot, Sir! I am innocent of this dreadful crime," he implored his interrogator.

For three days and nights Josef remained at the police station in appalling conditions, terrified that at any moment he would be summarily shot or hung. Finally, on the third day he was brought again before the interrogating officer.

Josef sat across the table from the officer who told him to lay his hands on the table in front of him and close his eyes. He did as he was told and immediately felt a burning pain on the back of his right hand as the officer stubbed out a cigarette on it. Josef screamed out in pain and jumped back in fright. The officer laughed. "Oh, you do have feelings, do you, German? I thought the Germans had no feelings. You must be a coward then. Put your hands on the table again," barked the interrogator. Once again Josef did as he was ordered, fearful of the outcome. "Close your eyes, pig," the officer ordered. Josef obeyed and immediately felt the agony of a hammer blow on the ends of two of his fingers on his left hand. This time Josef did not move his hand but opened his eyes and saw the pleasure in the eyes of his inquisitor opposite him.

"I hate you! I hate all of you Germans, and I have wanted to do that for a very long time," the officer said, his face distorted with anger and hate. "Now get out of here. We can find no evidence, but if I see you again, my report next time will be that you died in custody."

As Josef was about to leave the room, two junior soldiers entered. "Okay, okay! Sign this to say that you have been treated well whilst in detention and you can go," one of them said.

Josef painfully took the pen in his right hand and signed everything they put before him even though it was in Polish and he couldn't understand a word. Both his hands hurt like hell. He hoped he hadn't signed his own death warrant and that what he had signed wasn't a confession.

"Now clear off, German, and don't come back. We don't want any Germans here!"

They released Josef back onto the street with a hard kick to his backside that brought him to his knees. Painfully getting to his feet, he left the police station as quickly as he could. Perhaps even now they might change their minds, or worse still – they might actually discover some evidence against him.

Josef once more thanked God for his freedom. With a great sigh of relief, he continued his journey with as much haste as possible.

Chapter Nine - Tomasz

Painfully making his way along the road, Josef walked onto the bridge again and stood there staring at the river. Slowly getting his strength back, he decided it would be best to get out of the city at once. This was no longer friendly Breslau any more. It was unfriendly Wroclav. He was miles away in thought when he heard a voice speak to him in Polish. He looked around and replied that he was sorry but he was German, and didn't understand Polish.

"You look lost, my friend. Where are you going?" asked the stranger in German.

Josef was surprised at the friendliness of this young man, and replied that he was on his way back to Bavaria and the sooner he could get there the better. It was his home and he had been away for a long time. "So far," he added, "Poland hasn't been the friendliest of places."

The stranger introduced himself as Tomasz. He was a boyish, athletic-looking man of around 40, dressed very smartly in a dark grey suit, white shirt, grey tie and carrying a brown leather briefcase. He told Josef that he was a primary school teacher and lived and worked in the city. His mother had been German and his father Polish. When Silesia was taken from Germany and given to Poland, they were able to stay because of his father, unlike thousands of other ethnic Germans who had been forced to leave.

"The Germans were all just thrown out. Unfortunately, my father died soon after, in July 1945. It was always thought that his death was racially motivated. He was beaten up on his way home from work one day and died of his injuries. My mother died several years later of a broken heart; so I am here on my own now."

Tomasz looked down at Josef's hands and asked what had happened to them?
"I fell," Josef lied.

They chatted awhile before Tomasz suggested that they should walk back to his place to tend to Josef's hands.

"I can clean you up if you like and maybe you could stay for a bit of dinner?" he added. "I never really decided whether I should become a chef or a doctor, so I became a teacher instead," he said self mockingly with a smile. "I don't live far from here," he continued. "If you would like to come," he said pointing along the road.

Although at that moment Josef would rather have been on his own, and on his way, he agreed to this unusual show of kindness, and nodded his acceptance.

We can have a vodka and a chat if you like when you feel a bit better. It's nice for me to speak in German again," Tomasz said enthusiastically.

Tomasz led the way over the bridge and in no time at all, gestured ahead saying, "Here we are; my little home." Josef saw that Tomasz was pointing toward a non-descript, concrete tenement block right in the city centre, just a few minutes from where they had met. He led Josef up three flights of concrete stairs that hung precariously on the outside of the building. Reaching his front door, he unlocked it, and showed Josef in.

"It might not be much, but it is home to me," he said with a boyish smile. Josef commented that he thought it looked very comfortable and was quietly impressed with the little apartment. It seemed so clean and tidy, although there wasn't much decoration, or many personal touches. Obviously, Josef thought, there was no woman to brighten the place up.

Tomasz showed him over to a smart, brown leather settee and beckoned Josef to sit down asking him whether he would like a drink. Josef nodded and Tomasz quickly produced a bottle of vodka and two small glasses, which he placed on a round, glass-topped table in front of the settee. He filled two glasses, before sitting down beside Josef.

He took Josef's hands in his and looked at them. The nails of one hand were blackened and bruised, and the other hand showed a distinct sign of a burn mark.

"You tripped then?" Tomasz enquired doubtfully.

Josef repeated that he had fallen, as Tomasz tenderly dressed the burn with a bandage he produced from the little first aid box he had brought in with him from the kitchen.

When he finished the bandaging, he asked Josef if he would like another vodka. "It might take away some of the pain," Tomasz suggested thoughtfully.

After a nod from Josef, Tomasz poured the drinks for both of them. He was obviously pleased to share his drink and time with a fellow German speaker, Josef thought, and warmed to this honest show of friendliness and concern. Before picking up his drinks, Tomasz held Josef's bandaged hand and occasionally rubbed his fingers. Josef didn't think this particularly unusual, as Tomasz had shown so much concern for him since they had arrived at the apartment.

They both had so many questions to ask each other. Josef learned that the war had ended for Breslau on 6th May 1945, the city having been under siege for three months when the Gauleiter, Karl Hanke, surrendered to the Russians. This was only two days before the general surrender of the German Army to the Allies in Berlin on 8th May.

Tomasz said that it was estimated that 18,000 citizens had died during the siege.

"The refugees were from the lost Eastern territories," Tomasz said. "Twelve million of them were expelled from the old German lands. They headed west as 'displaced persons' to East Germany. Half a million never made it. The incoming Poles gave vent to their long stored-up hatred of the Germans, and they were treated with total callousness just like the Nazis treated the Poles when they dominated in the early years of the war. It would have been difficult at the time for the new local Polish population to see the Germans as victims, but that is what they had become after the war ended."

"East Germany? How many Germanys are there then?" Josef asked.

"Two," said Tomasz and explained that he was not joking. "Germany was divided into East and West at the end of the war."

"So where is Bavaria?" Josef asked.

"It's in the same place as it was when you were last there," Tomasz quipped with a smile.
"No! I mean East or West?" Josef questioned.

Tomasz knew what he meant and laughed, putting his hand on Josef's knee.

"It's in the West, Josef. It is in the American sector."

Josef thought for a moment saying that he understood now why Breslau was renamed Wroclaw. "It seems almost impossible that we could have lost the whole province, Tomasz."

Tomasz explained that besides Upper and Lower Silesia, Germany had also lost East Pomerania, some of Western Pomerania, East Prussia and East Brandenburg and everything else east of the Oder and Neisse rivers.

"In some respects," continued Tomasz, "It is a great tragedy when you think of the wonderful cities Germany lost; in East Prussia alone. "We, or should I say they," Tomasz corrected himself, as he was not sure if he were speaking as his mother's son or his father's. "We lost Königsberg, which is now a Russian enclave, as well as Allenstein, Marienburg, Memmel, Tilsit and many other smaller towns and cities," he said indignantly.

Tomasz continued, "It's called the Oder-Neisse Line. Basically the Germans lost everything east of those two rivers which run north and south."
"That is awful!" Josef said, adding, "It doesn't seem fair."

"It doesn't, I agree, but Germany lost the war and in consequence lost all those provinces. Germany's loss was Poland's gain. Mind you, the Russians held onto a lot of eastern Poland, which they had occupied in 1939. Perhaps we all just moved westward a bit."

"It's a split personality, Tomasz isn't it? You don't quite know whose side you are on?"

"I live and work here," Tomasz continued, "so I guess I am Polish. What do you think?" he said moving closer to Josef on the settee and rubbing Josef's knee.

Ignoring Tomasz, Josef said, "I think you are a Pole with a German trying to get out." They both laughed as Tomasz poured more vodka and put an arm around Josef's shoulder pulling him closer.

"Hitler was probably the most evil leader the world has ever known," Tomasz said. Basically, besides being born, he made three mistakes. First, he invaded Poland in 1939 which brought Great Britain into the war. Second, he invaded the USSR in 1941 – What a fool! As if the Germans could beat the Russians? And third, he declared war on the United States in January 1942. You've got to say he had some confidence, albeit misplaced. I would say he was a madman with delusions of grandeur!"

"And what about Stalingrad?" continued Tomasz, now in full swing. "He ordered his troops to stand firm in the face of an overwhelming onslaught from the Russians. That ended with a hundred thousand Germans being taken prisoner, including twenty-four generals. Didn't know much about tactics either, did he?"

"Well, he ruined my life, Tomasz," Josef said quietly. After a moment and still full of questions, Josef's thoughts returned to his home and he asked again about Bavaria and whether the Americans were occupying the country.

"Not any more. They are now on very good terms with the Federal Government of West Germany. The government is based in Bonn, and the president is Theodor Heuss. You should go there one day, Josef. They say it's a wonderful, picturesque little town on the Rhine. Or, of course," Tomasz said with a grin, "you could just stay here with me for a while?" he added.

"No, I couldn't do that. I need to get home, Tomasz. Please try to understand," he insisted, as they continued to sip the delicious vodka together. By now, the pair were both quite light-headed. "It was a tragedy, Josef, that so many German cities were all lost. Many had been seats of German learning for hundreds of years and all this has been taken from Germany." Tomasz sounded truly distraught over the loss.

"We lost the war, Tomasz," Josef said. "Perhaps it was the revenge of the victors."

"Have you heard of the Nemmesdorf massacre?" Tomasz asked. Josef shook his head.

"It was a massacre of civilians committed by the Russians in the last stages of the war. Nemmesdorf was one of the first villages taken by the Russians in Germany. They ran riot there. They killed most of the population. The women were stripped and raped then killed and nailed to doors in the crucifix position. There were bodies everywhere. The German army briefly retook the village and discovered the carnage. Such hate seems impossible to believe, but it happened."

"Beside the estimated seven million Germans killed in the war and the unparalleled devastation of German cities," Tomasz continued, "we lost the Eastern lands and much of our culture too. It was the same after the 1st World War. Again we lost land to the victors and 10% of the German lands were taken that time," Tomasz said, repeating himself.

"Mind you," he continued, "what they got were really just piles of ruins. All the cities had been flattened by the Soviets by the end of the war."

"But you said the Germans fled or were removed to the West?" Josef asked. "And I believe the German culture was in the people, not in the land or the rubble that was left. Everything just moved west – like Poland."

"Yes you are right, Josef, but after the war Germany was a land of old men, women and children, and those children, at least a third of them, had lost their fathers. They had a lot of work to do to get back on their feet as a nation. The West has been more successful than the East I have heard," Tomasz said.

Tomasz then suggested that they should eat something light. Josef agreed and Tomasz went off to prepare a snack. After a few minutes, he returned carrying a tray with two plates on it.

"I've made us a salad, Josef, as it's quite late and we don't want to eat too much at this time of night, do we?" Josef agreed and tucked into the food, with further glasses of vodka to wash it down.

When they finished, Tomasz suggested that Josef should stay the night.

"Can't throw you out now, can I? And anyway, I enjoy your company. You are a very stimulating person to be with," he added.

Josef was pleased to accept a night's lodgings as he was now very tired and a little drunk. He felt totally at ease with his new-found friend and stretched out on the comfortable sofa, as Tomasz went off to run the bath and prepare the bed.

When he returned, he beckoned Josef to come to the bathroom, where Josef stripped off his rags and noticed that Tomasz was studying him closely. Tomasz left the steamy bathroom as Josef climbed into the bath. He thought that the hot water was sensational and almost immediately fell asleep in the bath.

"Wake up, Josef," Tomasz said coming back into the bathroom. Josef, who had been dozing, stood up with a start to get out of the bath.

"You don't have to get out, Josef, sit back down and I will wash your back."

It was beautiful and Josef remembered how his wife Helma used to wash his back.

"There you are then Josef. All finished."

Josef slowly got out of the bath while Tomasz watched him dry himself. When he was finished, Tomasz peeled off his own clothes and got into the bath. "Can't afford two baths of water these days, Josef," he said with a grin.

By the time Tomasz had bathed and come into the bedroom, Josef was already in bed wearing the shorts Tomasz had loaned him. Tomasz stood by the bed naked for a moment, as though inviting Josef to look at him, before quickly jumping in beside him.

"Hope you don't mind, Josef. I always sleep like this." Josef didn't answer as he felt Tomasz cuddle up beside him.

To Tomas's surprise, Josef didn't protest, as he felt warm and somehow secure with Tomasz's body wrapped around him. It had been years since someone had shown him any affection, although this was the first time he had actually slept with another man and been this intimate.

He had, though, experienced plenty of other occasions with men in the camps, which had been a nightmare. The humiliation had been unbearable, a subject Josef could never talk about to anyone.

Male rape had been a daily occurrence in the camps in Russia. You couldn't resist the guards if you were "chosen" to be their plaything. You were marched into the guardhouse, ordered to strip, and lay over a table to be gang raped. It was best to just obey and think of something else. There was no point in thinking what was happening to you. You would soon have gone mad. The humiliation of it was appalling. Luckily for Josef, the men in most demand were those who had been in the Volkssturm defending Berlin. They had been boys at the end of the war and were, by then, handsome, virile young men. They were by far the most desirable prisoners for the guards, and were always chosen first. But those men had been repatriated early on, leaving the older prisoners to satisfy the lust of the guards in the later years.

Josef had heard of many cases of prisoners committing suicide because of the shame and humiliation of these attacks. Sometimes in his darkest moments he remembered the pain that had been excruciating as each guard took his turn to humiliate and overpower him. This wasn't only sexual; it was controlling. Many of the Russian guards had been away from their homes for months and didn't seem to care whom or what they violated.

Yet now Tomasz's arms were wrapped around Josef's body, which seemed completely different. He felt somehow happy and secure in his embrace as Josef drifted off into a sound, deep sleep and Tomasz, receiving no reply to a question from his partner, knew that Josef was asleep.

Tomasz held Josef's lean body all night, and they slept in late as it was the weekend. When he awoke, Tomasz was still wrapped around him as though preventing him from escape. But escape was never on Josef's mind. He had enjoyed the feel of an affectionate body beside him and strong arms wrapped around him. He had enjoyed physical contact again, a loving contact albeit with another man, and the closeness somehow felt beautiful to him.

They lay together in bed talking again for some while, Tomasz running his fingers through the few hairs Josef had on his chest. In total comfort, Josef lay there enjoying the contact.

"I have another question, Tomasz?" Josef said. "Did the Germans get to keep the Sudetenland?" They looked into each other eyes and began to laugh. The question seemed so out of place at that moment, but perhaps it was Josef just wanting to change the mood a little.

"What sort of question is that right now, Josef?"

Josef smiled. "I thought of it, so I decided I would ask it".

Tomasz gently ran his fingers across Josef's head of greying hair before answering. "No. they didn't. The Czechs took it back!"

"Oh, well! There goes Karlsbad too!" Josef said.

"Actually, Josef," Tomasz said with some authority, "It is now called Karlovy Vary.

"And another thing, Josef. It's strange really. The Germans call the territories ceded to Poland after the war Lost Lands while in Poland, we call them Recovered Territories. It's a question of perspective, isn't it?"

"There's the teacher coming out in you, Tomasz." Josef said smiling. Tomasz kissed Josef briefly on the neck and then tried to kiss him on the lips, but Josef resisted, turning his head. Being rejected, Tomasz jumped out of bed and invited Josef to take a shower with him. Josef quietly nodded his agreement.

They shared the shower together and dried each other. Afterwards, Tomasz suggested that he should sort out some of his wardrobe and find some new clothes for Josef, as they were both of a similar height.

"Mind you! I would rather see you like that," Tomasz joked looking at Josef with just a towel wrapped around his middle.

Bit by bit, Josef put on each item of clothing handed to him.

"I am so grateful to you, Tomasz! I do not have enough words to thank you," Josef said as he dressed in his new clothes.

"You look a new man, Josef, a very desirable one at that. Can't you stay with me a little longer?" Tomasz asked.

Josef felt such regret. Tomasz had been so good to him and he wished he could repay such kindness, but it was not possible. Regretfully, he explained that he must continue his journey home.

"I will never forget you, Tomasz. You have brought me back to life. It is almost like when I first met my wife. She roused my feelings and my emotions, but I have been dead inside all these last sixteen years until now." Josef saw tears in Tomasz's eyes. Tears of sadness? Tears of loneliness? Josef wasn't sure.

"If ever I get home, Tomasz, I will come back to see you one day." Josef promised."

Although he was grateful for the affection they had shared and he knew that Tomasz was lonely and needed a partner, Josef knew that he was not the one. No one could share his life but Helma and his family.

They embraced again, and Josef felt the same warmth and security in his friend's arms that he had felt during the night. He knew he had to leave. Yet somehow he felt guilty leaving Tomasz. He briefly considered that perhaps he should stay longer, perhaps a few more days. But no, he had to get home and each day longer that he stayed, the more difficult it would be for Tomasz to let him go, and harder for Josef to let him down. He felt sorry for Tomasz, but this lifestyle was not for him.

He gave Tomasz a final kiss on the neck and Tomasz, holding both Josef's ears gently, told him to shut his eyes and kissed him on the lips. Josef turned and hurried off. He didn't look back as he didn't want to see the tears in Tomasz's eyes.

Perhaps he didn't understand his own emotions at that moment, or perhaps they had just been re-awakened, after so many years of not experiencing any feelings of affection or closeness with another human being. Josef, without Helma, had been devoid of feelings. The war had closed off Josef's mind and heart to any feelings.

Now he had hope. To feel another human being close to him after all the past years was something foreign to him, and he had enjoyed being with Tomasz. He had blossomed in Tomasz's warmth and affection and had felt safe and secure in his arms. He had given as much of himself as he felt he could. Now he had to move on. He had to get home!

Chapter Ten - Anna

Josef left Tomasz and the city of Wroclav around lunchtime. He continued heading west with the warm sun on his back slowly making his way towards the border with East Germany. He followed the signs for Sroda Slaska, which was 32 km away with Legnica showing 60 km on a broken signpost that he past around mid afternoon.

He walked for a few hours, arriving at Sroda Slaska in the early evening. While in the little town, he asked in the bakery for some bread and was given two rather stale rolls that went down well with the ice-cold water from a drinking fountain in the nearby park. The jovial baker told him that in the German days the town had been called Neumarkt, but all the Germans had left at the end of the war in 1945.

Josef knew what that meant. The residents had been evicted forcibly from their homes and farms. He had heard this story so many times and felt sympathy for the victims each time he heard it. He understood that soldiers join or were conscripted into the army to fight and would not be welcome in foreign towns, but the civilians were defenceless and should not have been thrown out from where they may have lived for generations because of politics. He thought this was a wicked crime. What had happened to justice? Had it died at the end of the war, or was this the start of something new? The more he thought the more confused he felt.

"There was much violence," the baker continued. "Many Germans were killed before they could get away, it was a tragedy!" Josef didn't want to hear any more. He had lived through so much violence that he just didn't want to hear another story. He thanked the kindly baker for the bread, and after having his drink of water from the park, left the town feeling quite dispirited.

That night he slept in a wayside shrine just outside the town. Sleep came easily to him that night as he had walked a long way and was tired. He awoke early the next morning to the sound of traffic, and just lay there for awhile collecting his senses and listening to the different sounds. When he felt ready for the day, he got up, brushed himself down and started walking towards Legnica. He reached the town during the afternoon thanks to one short, bumpy ride in the back of a farm cart.

As he walked down the cobbled streets, he thought the town had a friendly feel about it, a cared-for feel. Tomasz, who had recommended it, said it was a nice town and he was right. There were flowerbeds everywhere and large pots of plants in front of most buildings. Geraniums hung in profusion from the many window boxes that decorated every windowsill. Josef noted, though, that much of the town was still in ruins.

Shortly, he came to a rather run-down, shabby looking guesthouse near the centre of town. It had no flowers outside and bombsites on either side of the building.

He went in and thought the bar looked somewhat dilapidated and in need of decoration. Nicotine darkened timber beams supported the low wooden ceiling, and there were many dusty woodcarvings hanging on the walls; among them was a Madonna, a crucifix, and a mountain scene with the word Silesia on a scroll at the bottom. It reminded him of an Alpine inn.

He took a seat by the window that looked out onto the picturesque little square. Tomasz had given him some money to last a few days, so he was able to order a small lunch.

A middle-aged, elegant woman some years older than himself served him. Although she looked tired, she was still a very handsome woman. She was dressed all in grey with a clean white, pressed apron around her waist. She had blond hair going grey that was pulled back and hung in two long plaits at the back of her head. Josef ordered a small lunch of sauerkraut, sausage meat and black bread. The meal, when it came, was delicious and he swilled it down with a cool beer. He thought the nearer he came to Germany, the better the beer tasted.

When he had finished his meal, the woman who had served him came to sit down opposite him at the table, and began to speak to him in German.

"You are German, aren't you?" she asked, confirming her suspicions.

"Yes, I am," he said after a long pause.

"I can tell," she said. "My husband was also German," she continued. "My name is Anna. At the end of the war with my husband gone and my mother being Polish, we were allowed to stay on here. Many, of course, the ethnic Germans, were thrown out of their homes and off their land and put on buses to Germany. We were the lucky ones."

Josef stared deeply into her stony grey eyes but saw nothing. He was expecting perhaps to see some peace, some understanding maybe even some fun, but nothing showed through but sadness. She had tired eyes set in an expressionless, gaunt face.

"My life hasn't been easy," she said. "My Ernst was killed in the war, and I have lived here ever since with my mother who is now quite old and sick." Feeling somewhat uncomfortable, Josef changed the subject asking, "How far is it to the border?"

"Not far, maybe 80 kilometres. I am not sure as I have never been there," she answered.

"Perhaps you should go one day," Josef responded kindly.

"No, not now," she replied. "I have to run the guesthouse, and my mother needs me."

Josef suddenly felt a great sorrow for Anna. In a way, she too, had been imprisoned all these years. The war had ruined her life and she was a prisoner, not as he had been, but a prisoner of the war all the same, a prisoner and a victim.

Josef got up from the table when he had finished his meal and sat on a nearby settee. He was hoping Anna would not mind if he rested a bit before continuing his journey. He was so weary and the meal had made him quite sleepy. "Of course you can have a little nap if you like," Anna said. "You look so tired." Gratefully, Josef removed his shoes and stretched out on the settee and soon fell asleep. He had walked just under 30km that day.

While he slept, he dreamt of orders being shouted at him above the sound of explosions, and of his ever-present fear of dying. His dreams were often like that even though the war had been over for ten years, it was still very fresh in his mind. For him it had never really ended.

When he awoke it was dark. He saw in the candlelight, that the hands on the wooden clock on the mantle piece pointed to 9. "That was a nice sleep," Anna said quietly. Startled he looked around and saw her sitting nearby watching him.

"Yes, it was! Thank you for letting me have a sleep. You should have woken me up earlier and thrown me out," he smiled.

"No, no!" she said. "I would never throw you out. You are a war hero and a guest. And remember what they say 'the guest is king.'"

Josef ignored the compliment. He certainly didn't feel a hero. He was only a farmer from Bavaria who had become mixed up in a ghastly war, and now just wanted to get home to resume his life. He stood up and looked out of the window. It was raining and dark. Anna came up and stood close behind him.

"You had better stay here the night," she said. "I can't let you go off in this weather."

Josef thanked her for her kindness saying that he was grateful for the offer and would be glad to pay her. He would leave early the next morning. Anna locked up for the night as there were no customers.

They sat down together and Anna turned the radio on and they listened to Viennese music: Tales From The Vienna Woods, The Blue Danube and

The Kaiser Waltz. They both loved that sort of music. Josef felt quite light-headed and nearly asked Anna to dance, but he knew that would have been a bit presumptuous at this point. Finally, when the broadcast ended, Anna stood up, went over to the radio and switched it off.

"It is time for bed now, Josef. I will show you to your room first, and then I will attend to my mother," she said leading the way up the rickety wooden stairs lit only by the candle she held rather unsteadily in her hand.

Josef's room, which was next to Anna's, also reminded him of the Bavarian style; lots of pine fittings and furniture with two large wooden beds pushed together in the middle with a white eiderdown quilt turned sideways on each bed.

"Good night then, and God Bless you," Anna said as she left him and went along the hall to her mother's room.

Pouring cold water from a large jug into a china bowl on a stand, Josef washed and dried himself on the clean white hand towel that was placed neatly nearby. He got into bed and was soon asleep. Sleep, as always, seemed to come easy to him. He dreamed of his beautiful farm in Sparneck, and Helma, his wife, there in the dairy milking the cows with their two young boys helping her.

He must have slept for a couple of hours, when he was awakened from his sleep by Anna, who had snuggled up beside him in his bed.

"I was cold," she said apologetically. Suddenly, she sat up, removed her nightdress and lay down again beside him. Josef turned over and put his arm around her to warm her, but realised she was already very warm. Her large breasts pressed into his bare chest as they both pushed their naked bodies closer together. Josef moved to lie on top of her and it felt good as they made love without a word being spoken.

Anna's breath came short and sharp and she let out little screams of pleasure as she reached her numerous climaxes. Joseph stayed quiet, as he too was finally satisfied. Anna had resisted his kisses but she seemed to love being loved. She relished the feeling of a man deep inside her after all these years, and Josef was a man. He was a big man who, like her, had many years of loving to make up for.

They lay side by side for a short while savouring their time together. At last Anna said without embarrassment, "Thank you, Josef. That was beautiful." She then got out of bed, wished him good night again, and silently went back to her own room.

Surprisingly, Josef was grateful for the gift of her body, which she had given so freely and completely. They had both been starved of love and affection for so long that this ultimate act was an affirmation of the good in humanity for both of them.

He slept late the following morning, and it was only when he heard Anna's mother calling for her, and Anna moving around in the next room, that he woke up. After attending to her mother, Anna came back into his room, slipped off her dressing gown and once again climbed into his bed. Even more comfortable with each other, they repeated their lovemaking. This time, Josef lay on his back as Anna slowly lowered herself onto her prize and rocked backwards and forwards for a while before lifting herself up and down as she rode Josef like a horse. She let out muffled screams as she felt the full force of Josef deep inside of her. They both craved sex, not love, but sex for its own sake, because they had been so long without it. When they were both completely satisfied, Anna got out of bed, and wrapped her dressing gown around her. "Thank you again Josef," she said smiling shyly, "That was both beautiful and wonderful."

"Yes, it was, but I should be thanking you," he replied. "You made me very happy."

"Let's just say it was a gift we could give to each other, Josef," she said.

Anna left him in bed and returned to her own room. He slowly got out of bed and washed.

When he left his room, he looked in at Anna's door. She was dressing and looked slightly embarrassed when she saw he was admiring her. "You are a fine lady, Anna," he said. She smiled at him, and thanked him. Turning towards him with her stocking still in her hand, she gestured for him to go.

They ate a late breakfast together and sat chatting about her mother, the weather, and her business. As they ate their breakfast together, they continued to enjoy simple conversation. She obviously liked his company, and he enjoyed being with her. Yet at the back of his mind, he knew he had to continue his journey as soon as possible. He could not stay longer with her. After so many years, he just needed to get home.

When he told Anna his intentions, she began to cry. "Please just stay a little while with me, Josef. Please! I need you?"

At first, he didn't know what to do but finally said, "Perhaps I could stay another night if I can do some work for you today as a thank you for your hospitality."

Anna smiled. "Thank you, Josef. You are a very caring and understanding man. You don't know me too well, but you understand me. We understand each other. That is so wonderful. Your wife is a very lucky woman," she said. Josef just nodded.

Josef worked hard that day, mainly in the garden and later in the cellar where he was surprised to find many pre-war bottles of wine. He looked at the labels and took one back upstairs with him.

"There must be a fortune in vintage wine in your cellar, Anna," he told her, showing her the bottle. he had picked out for them to enjoy.

By lunchtime, a gorgeous smell of sauerkraut pervaded the whole house. "It's sauerkraut and Bockwurst with something else special in it," Anna said.

"Well, whatever it is, it smells delicious," he answered.

"I will surprise you then, Josef," she said. "I mean with the dinner," she said shyly casting her eyes down.

"You already have," he answered with a smile.

After lunch, which included pieces of ham in the sauerkraut, a speciality in those parts, Josef went out into the garden to repair the fence. He remembered repairing another fence some weeks earlier in the Ukraine in the Soviet Union, before he had made his escape from the old peasant. Even though the time had passed so quickly, it all seemed a very long time ago in a different world and a different time. But the thought made Josef realise he was still a long way from home.

That evening, as Anna prepared another meal, Josef opened the bottle of wine he had found in the cellar earlier in the day. They sat together at the scrubbed pine table across from each other and ate the beautiful meal she had prepared. This time it was Wiener Schnitzel with potatoes and the remainder of the lunchtime sauerkraut. Two candles burned in the middle of the table, and they each had a glass of wine before them. It seemed so romantic to them both, and a preparation for what was to come later.

After dinner, they walked for a while outside, but the night air was chilly and damp so they went back into the house after just a short time. Once again, they played music on the radio and their minds were both transported back to another world, a world before the war when everything seemed so easy, so calm and so peaceful.

They slept together again that night and repeated their love making a number of times. It was beautiful for both of them. They slept in late again the next morning, and were only roused when, Anna's mother woke them with her calls.

Anna left the bedroom to attend her mother, while Josef washed and dressed and went out onto the landing to go downstairs. As he passed Anna's room, he looked in to see if she was there but the room was empty. He was surprised to see a picture on the wall of a man dressed in the uniform of the Gestapo.

At that moment, Anna came out of her mother's room and asked what he was doing in her room? Embarrassed at being found there, he said, "Actually I was looking at that picture. Who is he?" he enquired.

"It's Ernst, my husband. He was always a good man to me," she said defensively. "We were married for ten years," she continued. "We had no children, it just never happened. After the war, they took him away." Anna looked away unable to continue.

"Who?" asked Josef. "He was in the Gestapo by the look of it?" His question sounded more like a statement of recrimination.

"Yes, he was," she answered, eyes cast down. "But he was the kindest, gentlest man I have ever known. He wouldn't hurt anyone. After the war, he came home to work again in the business. Then one day a year or so after his return, Russian soldiers came for him, and he was arrested. They took him to Nuremberg, tried him, and found him guilty of many murders. He appealed but they hung him anyway."

"At the time the Russians came," she continued tearfully, "we were fighting being expelled to the West, as my mother was Polish and wanted to stay here. Had we gone, we would have lost everything. All alone, I had to cope with the death of my husband and the extradition proceedings at the same time. It was awful," she said. "Staying or going would not have effected by husband's position. He was on the wanted list of the Allies and that was it."

She looked away and continued. "If we had had children it might have been bearable, but I was on my own with my mother. From the day when he was arrested, I have had to bear the unbearable."

Anna sat on the bed, hung her head and sobbed uncontrollably. Josef sat beside her, putting a comforting arm around her shoulder, but it didn't help as she just pushed him away.

"It's been nine years now since they took him, and I miss him so much every day."

"I can imagine," Josef replied.

"I rent out the fields and run the pub, but I make nothing, just enough to live on."

Josef felt real sadness for Anna but not for Ernst her dead husband. He knew by reputation how brutal and ruthless the Gestapo had been. He had seen it with his own eyes and had feared them himself.

"The Gestapo were scum, emotionally dead, Anna, and they acted like wild animals. They were the lowest of the low."

He had said out loud his thoughts and immediately knew he had said too much. He corrected himself quickly but he had said it. "I mean!" he started to say. Suddenly he saw Anna's face and fell silent. She scowled at him and her face went white.

"How can you say that? To me he was a wonderful man. He was my husband. You will never understand. And you? I don't think you are even fit to shine his boots." Josef felt shocked at her reaction. Her bitterness even after all these years surprised him.

Standing up, she said, "I think you had better go now. I have nothing more to say to you.
Please go. It was very nice having you here, but I want you to go. I really am alone now," she said breaking down in tears again.

Josef stood up, and said goodbye quickly without looking at her. He gathered his few belongings and left Anna crying. He felt ashamed for his mistake. It may have been true what he said, but he should not have said it the way he did.

As he left the house, he turned and called out "Anna!" But she had already shut the door.

"What a fool I am!" he said out loud. She had given him her hospitality, love and affection and he had abused it. He felt ashamed! She had only known her husband as a loving man, and not as the hateful Gestapo soldier he was, or had to be, during the war.

Josef sadly left the shabby, run-down guesthouse in Legnica and headed down the High Street in the direction of Görlitz, Germany, – and home! As he came to the last house in the town, he wondered whether he should go back and try to make his peace with Anna, to console her for her loss, and to apologise for his rudeness. But as he stopped to deliberate, a horse-drawn farm cart came up alongside him.

An old man with a very wrinkled, brown, smiley face, said something to him in Polish.

Josef looked at the friendly old man and said, "German, sorry. No Polish."

"Ah so!" replied the Pole in German. "So you are German? Would you like a lift?"

"Yes, please," replied Josef. "Where are you going?"

The farmer said that he was going to the next village, Lubiatow. "You people called it Lobendau, when it was in Germany," he said with a smile. Josef jumped aboard and they hit the road west at all of ten miles an hour.

The farmer spoke quite good German and they were able to converse fairly well. He told Josef that the majority of older people could understand some German still.

Josef told the old man that he had stayed two days at the Black Prince Guesthouse run by Anna, the owner, but had left after a misunderstanding.

"Ah, Anna, a very sad lady who lost her husband in the war," said the old man.

"I understood it was after the war," replied Josef.

"Ah so! You know then? Her husband, that bastard, Ernst! He came home here after the war and just carried on his normal life for a time. Then one day, a group of Russian soldiers came and arrested him. He protested his innocence the whole time. He said he only acted on orders, and that it was all part of a big plan, and he was only a small cog. Anyway, in the end the allies executed him for his crimes. You wouldn't believe the things they said he did?"

Eager to tell Josef more, he went on, "He was stationed at Auschwitz for about two years. You know it's only down the road really. During the week, he would be a part of the killing process at the camp, and most weekends he would return home here as if nothing had happened. It was as though he were a bank manager or something, not a mass murderer."

"It is said he killed lots of people personally with his own gun. He deserved everything he got, the swine. Mind you, it must have been terrible for Anna, not knowing what was going to happen. She thought he had some sort of office job at the camp. We all felt so sorry for her. She withdrew from village life and still, all these years later, is still a very private person. She just can't come to terms with the fact that her husband was a brute, a mass murderer."

Josef left it there. What was there to say? It was all in the past, a long time ago and he didn't want to get into that sort of discussion. The magnitude of the crimes committed by the Nazis, done in the name of the German people, was only just beginning to sink in as far as he was concerned.

"You know," continued the old Pole, "most people around here were of the opinion that, 'The only good German was a dead German.' Looking back, there was no point in trying to explain that there were good people as well as bad people in every nation. The Poles really suffered under the Nazis and perhaps this was their only chance to get their own back. So when the war was over, the Poles gave the ethnic Germans a really hard time around here."

The old Pole thought for a moment before continuing. "I don't know what's right or wrong anymore. It was all a long time ago. Luckily, I have a Polish surname and am a second generation

Pole, so the evictions didn't affect me although I lost a number of good friends. It was a terrible end to a terrible time for both the German and Polish people."

What could Josef say to this friendly old Pole? Sorry? No, it was best to remain silent.

"Where are you from in Germany?" the old man asked. Josef told him that he was from the Hof area of Bavaria. The old Pole looked amazed. "I had family there before the war on my mother's side. They used to take me for picnics up the Waldstein Mountain. Do you know it? It's a wonderful place to go," he said.

"Yes, I do," Josef said surprised. "Do you remember the Bear Trap on the mountain?"

The old Pole smiled and nodded. "That brings back memories of my youth."

"And the old castle up there," the old Pole continued. "What a look-out position that was! Can't remember what it was called."

"The Great Waldstein, the Red Castle," Josef interjected. "And the look-out point is the Schussel Observation Pavilion?"
"Yes, I remember. We ran there once to shelter from the rain. Up there on that mountain is the source of the Saxon Saale River, did you know that?" The old Pole asked, quite excitedly. Josef

nodded but didn't answer. He just fell silent, deep in thought of all those wonderful places associated with home and his life before the war.

After about an hour or so, the old man told Josef that he had reached his destination. He winked and said, "Germany is just down the road," pointing to the west. "Farewell and good luck, my friend, and thank you so much for reminding me of my past. As Josef started to climb down from the cart, the old man stopped him. Thinking a moment, the old man turned back to Josef. Before you go, why not share my lunch with me?"

Josef nodded gratefully and watched as the old Pole opened a green cloth napkin to reveal a large bread roll filled with salami and cheese, which he offered to share with him. Josef thanked him and smiled. They sat chatting as they ate and when they had finished, Josef climbed from the cart. As he did so, he noticed a pall of smoke over the town of Legnica that they had only left an hour or so previously. A dreadful thought came over Josef and a feeling of horror of what it might be.

"Would it be possible to take me back into the town?" Josef asked the old man.

Seeing the panic in Josef's eyes the old Pole replied, "Of course, climb back in." Josef jumped back in, and the cart was turned around, and they headed back as fast as they could into town. As they drew near Josef's stomach began to turn over, and the hair on his arms stood on end.

When they arrived back in the town, Josef's worse suspicions were realised as he saw Anna's guest house, now just a smouldering ruin. There didn't seem to be much left at all, as the building had been constructed mostly of wood. Jumping from the cart he began running towards the fire. But as he got nearer, the tremendous heat the smouldering ruin gave off forced him back. He just could not get near it.

There was a small fire engine, two police cars and an ambulance at the scene. The old Pole who had brought Josef back in to town asked an elderly policeman, who stood with a grim face in front of the still burning embers, if there were any survivors? The policeman stared at the ground and shook his head. He muttered sadly that he had known both the occupants well.

"Lovely people, tragic people, but they are both gone now. It's one more disaster for our little town," he said, almost in tears. "But why?" he continued, "We will never know what happened?"

But Josef knew! He knew that he had shown Anna another life, a better life only to snatch it away from her so suddenly. He had let her down, and then left her. She had felt abandoned as if there were nothing left to live for. Josef didn't even want to think of her last moments, how she and her mother must have suffered, as the flames consumed them.

Thanking the old Pole once again for his kindness, Josef left the town of Legnica on foot with tears in his eyes and his head bowed very low. He was overcome with sorrow. He wished that he had never come into Anna's life.

Chapter Eleven - Hospitalised

It was mid afternoon when Josef left Legnica for the second time that day, and the sun was really hot in a clear blue sky. Lobendau was to the north and an old sign indicated that the next town on his way back to Bavaria was Bolesawiec, some twenty kilometres further. In the south, he could still see the Sudeten Mountains known as the Giant Mountains to Josef when he was a child. He remembered this area had sparked a world crisis before the war.

The Sudetenland had been annexed by Germany in 1938 on the pretext that the area was mostly German speaking. That seemed reasonable to him, but the rest of Czechoslovakia had followed not long after, and Josef knew that was wrong.

He made a great effort to walk faster; refreshed as he was with the good food he had had during the previous few days. He reached his destination, Bolesawiec, at dusk and made for a bus shelter by the river.

He saw the name of the river on a signboard, which surprised him as it also included its German name, the Bober River. The sign stated that it was a tributary of the Oder River. Josef knew the Oder River. He was nearing home at last, he thought.

He slept well in the bus shelter that night and dreamed of his father telling him how, at the end of the First World War, the Kaiser, Wilhelm II, had been deposed and gone into exile in Holland. The Kaiser had been lucky that the queen of the Netherlands, Queen Wilhelmina had given him sanctuary.

The Kaiser was allowed to live out the rest of his days in some splendour, like a country gentleman at his mansion in Doorn. He had purchased the property in 1919, following his abdication, and died there in 1941. On the other hand, King George V of England had refused permission for the Russian royal family to settle in England, and the Bolsheviks had killed the entire family. "Lucky Wilhelm, unlucky Nicholas and his family," Josef thought to himself.

It was already quite light when he woke from his dreams the next morning. He felt a bit damp and stiff, but he knew that once he got going and the sun warmed up, he would be fine. He had breakfast from a street food seller in the pretty town square before continuing on his way. As he ate, he thought back to Breslau and Tomasz, and his generosity in giving him money for his journey. He was just on the western outskirts of the town when he began to feel unwell with nausea and stomach pains.

Sitting down by the side of the road, he all at once began to vomit. His stomach heaved and ached, and he was disturbed to see that he was also bringing up some blood. He hailed a passing cart and asked the driver if he would be so kind as to take him back into the town.

The driver of the cart, seeing that Josef was so unwell, took pity on him and delivered him directly to the local doctor. After doing a few tests, the doctor said that he was suffering from food poisoning. Josef would have to go to the nearest hospital that was in Zgorzelec, some thirty kilometres away.

The doctor called an ambulance which seemed to take forever to arrive, while Josef continued to retch and vomit. When the ambulance finally arrived, Josef saw that it was not so much an ambulance as a converted American jeep. The driver loaded a very sick Josef on board, and drove like a madman, to the hospital. When they arrived, the driver told him that they had made the journey in record time. "Never been so fast," the driver boasted cheerily. Josef just stared up to the sky unable to respond to anything.

After Josef had been at the hospital a short while, an orderly told him to sit on a chair facing the toilet. The orderly then gave him a glass of salt water to drink, which induced more vomiting. Josef had thought there was nothing left in his stomach to come up, but then discovered how wrong he had been. He felt so very sick and weak and he knew he had a very high temperature. He thought he was near to death.

Even though he felt so unwell, he was comforted to learn that he was in a town on the eastern side of the Neisse River. On the other side was Görlitz in Germany, so if he should die now, he had almost made it home. At the end of the Second World War, the town had been divided, the eastern side becoming part of Poland and renamed Zgorzelec, and the western side remaining German. He only had to cross the narrow river, and he would be in Germany! He realised that he could be home in a few days if he survived, but at that moment he had his doubts.

He lay in the hospital very sick for three days sometimes shivering, sometimes sweating profusely, all the time drifting in and out of consciousness. He kept imagining he was with his father's two brothers on a First World War battlefield. Both the brothers had been killed in the war, and their names were remembered on the war memorial in the little village of Mödlareuth in Bavaria, which Josef and his parents often visited before the war.

He was only given water on in the first few days of his confinement, but on the third day he had some soup. As he lay in the bed, feeling better, he slowly became aware of a catheter bag protruding from the left side of the bed. He hated the thought of that bag, but accepted that it was necessary.

On the fourth day, he began to feel a little better as his health improved and he was able to sit up and take some solid food. In the afternoon of the fourth day, his catheter was removed, which made him feel a whole lot more comfortable. He was allowed to get out of bed and walk about, even though he still felt very weak and kept coming over faint.

In the bed next to him was a man who coughed a lot. He told Josef that he had been born German and was from the eastern side of the city. At the end of the war he had come home to find that his small-holding was in Poland and unless he took Polish citizenship he would be thrown out. He was now Polish by name! He winked and said. "By name only, my friend!" Josef chuckled, and felt a whole lot better.

"The war changed so many people's lives around here," the old man said, "but at least we survived. Of course," he went on, "when the Eastern provinces of Germany were given to Poland, ethnic Germans were forcibly moved out to the west and the new German borders. Their homes and lands were given to Poles. In turn, many of the Poles who took over those lands had been evicted by the Russians in the east from their homes which had been incorporated into Russia."

"The Germans didn't only lose the war, my friend, around these parts they also lost the peace as their lands and possessions were taken from them and they were thrown out of the country," the old man said. "It turned out quite lucky for me though," he continued. "As a plumber, because they needed the tradesmen, I was allowed to stay on here with my wife who was Polish. I took Polish citizenship and was not thrown out of my home to become a refugee in Germany."

Josef didn't answer the man; he just listened. He had learned it was better to stay silent on political and controversial issues.

Josef had heard a similar story before from Tomasz in Breslau, or rather Wroclav, and realised there was still a lot of resentment on the subject. The transfer of Silesia, agreed at Potsdam by the Allied leaders, even before the war ended, seemed to have been a disaster. Communities were uprooted and people thrown out of their homes and off lands that some had lived on for centuries.

Josef told the old man that he was glad that things had turned out well for him and hoped he would soon be well again.

On the fifth day of his stay in the hospital, he was told that he was being released. Although he still felt weak, he had been well cared for and was glad to be able to continue his journey home. He said good-bye to those he was leaving behind in the ward, and left the hospital after lunch.

169

He walked down the steps of the hospital and asked the doorman the directions to the river. Pointing to his right, the man told him it was only a short walk away. He hurriedly walked along the road till he came to a T-junction. On the other side of the road he saw the narrow Neisse River, and realised that Germany was only a few metres away now. However, he could not see a bridge over the river. He looked to the left and right but no bridge was in sight.

He stopped a passer-by and said "Germany?" The raggedly dressed pedestrian ignored him and just kept walking. He tried again a little later and an old lady pointed her stick to the right. Josef thanked her and began to walk in the direction the old lady had directed him.

It must have taken an hour or more before he saw a bridge a kilometre or so ahead of him. The river widened at this point and as Josef approached the bridge, he could see guards manning both sides checking papers.

He could feel his heart pounding as he approached the Polish guards. He got out his release paper to show them, but they pushed him back. "No Go! All finish for today." Josef showed his paper again and was again pushed back.

"Border closed for today. You go away. Come back tomorrow." Josef didn't argue. He knew that would be useless. He left the area of the bridge immediately, and made his way back into town and sat in a bus shelter wondering what to do.

It was late afternoon, and he watched as the people left their jobs in the town centre to go home. It looked like he was there for the night, but hoped that he would be able to cross into Germany the next day. As he looked around the town square, he saw an elderly gentleman beside his ancient Mercedes car. "Can you help me please?" the elderly gentleman asked in some distress, motioning to Josef.

"I don't understand. I am sorry," Josef replied .

"Oh, you are German?" said the elderly gentleman in German. "Maybe you can help me? My car won't start. Do you know anything about the workings of a motor?"

"Actually, before the war, I did most of the repairs on our tractor. I am a farmer," Josef said rather reflectively.

"Oh, that's good! So I have found the best person available, have I?" The elderly gentleman said with a smile.

"Raise the bonnet. Let us take a look," replied Josef.

After a little while, Josef reappeared from under the bonnet and smiled at the gentleman.

"Where's the starting handle?" Josef asked.

"Here," the elderly gentleman said, handing it to Josef.

Josef inserted the handle into the engine at the front of the car. "Give it some choke," Josef asked. Josef then gave the starter handle a few turns, and the engine immediately burst into life.

"That is wonderful Sir! Thank you. By the way, my name is Stefan," added the gentleman.

"Nice to meet you," Josef said shaking Stefan's hand. "And my name is Josef."

Stefan enquired as to what Josef was doing in the town. When Josef had finished telling his story, Stefan said, "You can stay the night with my wife and me. We would be pleased to have you stay with us after you have been so helpful."

Josef happily got into Stefan's car, and they sped off in an easterly direction. After about ten minutes, Stefan pointed ahead saying "Here we are." Josef saw a cluster of farm buildings, and set apart from them was what looked like a large old barn with ancient exposed timbers decorating the outside.

"That's an old building," observed Josef.

"Yes, it's all that is left of the family castle that stood over there," said Stefan, pointing to a pile of old tumbled down walls to the left of the barn. "Of course, my family were very grand once. We were Szlachtas. The word you use in German is Junker, the ruling aristocracy. We were the land owning class. Sadly there isn't much left of the property now, and since 1921 all our privileges have been abolished. My family name is Zamojshi. We were well bred and owned all of the land around here. The land now belongs to the State and we, that is my wife and I, only have the barn that once served as the mews for the castle."

Stefan showed Josef into the spacious building and introduced him to his wife, Maria. Later there followed a beautiful meal during which Stefan explained that he had three sons, two in West Germany and one in New York. After an enjoyable evening, Josef was given a warm bed for the night. Josef was pleased he had been able to help this old gentleman, and secure himself accommodation for the night.

The following morning after a good breakfast, Josef said his good-byes to his hosts and headed back into town whistling loudly. He was pleased that finally he would soon cross back over the border into Germany. It had been so many years!

Chapter Twelve - Arrival in Germany

It took Josef about an hour to walk back into town. He was feeling fine after his meal the night before, and his breakfast earlier. He was looking forward to finally crossing the border back into Germany. Since the end of the war, as Tomasz had told him, the Oder and Neisse Rivers had been the border between Poland and East Germany.

Josef cautiously made his way directly to the bridge. He showed his paper to the Polish border guards. This was the paper he had received from the prison camp confirming that he had been a prisoner of war in Russia for ten years. The guards hardly glanced at the grubby piece of paper and beckoned him on. He hesitantly crossed the narrow river and hailed the two guards who stood on the other side waiting for him. He noticed somewhat disconcertingly that they both had red stars on their fur hats.

"Hallo," he said, "I have come home after ten years in a Russian prison. I was a prisoner-of war." The guards did not reply but one walked casually to a phone that hung on the side of the guard's pillbox. The guard picked up the 'phone and, with his back turned to Josef, made a call.

Josef couldn't quite hear what was being said as the guard spoke in a whisper. When he had finished, he turned to Josef and said, "You must wait here, Russkie."

"No, I am German from Bavaria. My name is Josef Holz," he said. "I was a prisoner of the Russians," adding as an afterthought, "for ten years."

He was left waiting for some hours sitting slumped against the side of the pillbox, until an army jeep arrived with uniformed officers inside. "Climb in," ordered an officer, and Josef obeyed, getting into the back seat of the vehicle next to a guard with a sub-machine gun resting on his lap. He looked suspiciously at Josef and frowned, saying something under his breath.

"Where are you taking me? I have come home." Josef said in a somewhat subdued voice. No one answered and the vehicle sped on for over an hour till he saw a sign showing that Dresden was three kilometres ahead.

At this point, the vehicle made a sharp left turn and within a few moments was speeding through the gates of some sort of barracks, the brick and stone type built before the war during the time of the National Socialists. Josef thought how dismal and foreboding it looked.

The vehicle came to an abrupt stop, and he was ordered to get out and follow the officer. The guard with the sub-machine gun followed cautiously at the rear of the group, into the threatening looking building.

Josef was taken into a holding room where the door was shut and locked with a loud thud, and he was left on his own. If this were his welcome home, it was not a very good start. He had succeeded in making the difficult journey back to Germany that had taken months and at times been very dangerous, only to be held a prisoner in his own country.

It was dark before he heard the door being unlocked, and an officer entered the room.

"So!" the officer said, "Tell me your story!"

Josef related most of the things he could think of that had happened to him since his release from the prison camp in Russia. This took some time, and the officer kept looking at his watch and appeared irritated. "Okay, okay! I will check your story. In the meantime, you will have to remain here." With that he got up and left the room. The door was once again locked from the outside leaving Josef to spend an uncomfortable night in the cell.

Sitting on the floor of the little cell, he began to panic. After all he had gone through to be imprisoned again in his own country? He could not believe it. Why hadn't he been welcomed as a long lost hero? Where were the handshakes, the flags, and the marching bands? There was nothing but suspicion and distrust, and now he was locked up again.

He finally fell asleep but woke early the following morning when a uniformed guard brought him some coffee and rye bread.

"Why am I still here?" he asked the guard. The guard ignored the question and left the cell without speaking.

A little later, the door was once again opened and he was escorted to an interview room that was full of cigarette smoke.

"Sit down!" ordered the civilian official. He offered Josef a cigarette, which Josef declined. The official looked long and hard at Josef before saying, "Who are you and where are you from? This rubbish about Russia really is unbelievable. You are a liar. Tell the truth and maybe I will be able to make things easier for you. You are either a traitor or a criminal."

Josef hid his head in his hands and just stayed silent. If they would not believe the truth there was nothing more he could say.

Suddenly the inquisitor stood up, walked around behind Josef, and yanked him by the hair so forcefully that he tumbled back over his chair. Bringing his face close to Josef's he shouted, "If you don't tell me what I want to know, you will never leave this building alive."

Josef told his story again, about the last days in Berlin, his capture and transportation to the Soviet Union. About the years of toil in the mines and finally, after all the years, his release and journey home. He had told his story so many times that he remembered the details well. Sometimes it was hard to tell and to relive, as he spoke of all the indignities and brutalities he had suffered. He just wanted to forget, not remember.

The official looked at him with a scowl and screamed, "Liar!"

The guards were called and Josef was, once again escorted to the cell and roughly thrown in. He sat on the wooden board, which also served as a bed. Tears began to run down his cheeks. He buried his face in his hands and cried silently.

Some hours later the process was repeated again but with another official equally as threatening. Josef repeated his story once again. "Can't you see," the interrogator insisted, "you will die in here if you don't tell the truth?" You are a fool and you will never see your family again and do you know what? - I don't care!" With that he left the room slamming the heavy door behind him.

These interviews continued throughout the night and into the next day. Between the interviews, loud music was introduced into his cell from an old speaker fitted high up on the wall. The sound of the music was deafening and Josef lay on his side on the wooden bed with his fingers in his ears trying to shut out the noise.

As suddenly as it had started, after many hours, it went silent. The music was switched off. He had lost all sense of time and reason. He found the silence deafening and heard a loud whistling in his ears. Hours later, two guards came into the cell and told him to strip to the waist and kneel down. He obeyed the order and saw the bigger of the two guards produce a riding crop. He beat Josef around the neck and shoulders shouting, "Talk, you bastard." Josef screamed with pain and, fell to the floor. He tried to get up but was unable to do so as the beating continued.

After awhile the guards finally left the cell. Josef lay in great pain with a feeling of utter hopelessness and despair.

Many more hours passed before two new, young guards entered the cell. "You will sign this statement, and then we will see what we can do for you," said one of them. They gave Josef back his shirt and he was ordered to follow one of the guards with the other one close behind him. Back in the interview room, they ordered Josef to sit down at the table.

An official provided pen and paper for him to make his written statement. Suddenly, Josef remembered his capture in the ruins of Berlin. He had been dragged by the collar from the cellar where he had taken cover and been thrown into the back of an armoured vehicle as bombs were exploding all around him. It had been hell on earth. Now his return to his homeland seemed another hell on earth.

He wrote for some time, until he felt his statement was as complete, but omitted the events with the hunter in Poland. He handed it to one of the guards who glanced at it quickly and handed it back to him.

"You will also state that you insulted the German Democratic Republic and were beaten up by an angry crowd. Then you can leave."

Josef did as he was told. He wrote on a fresh piece of paper knowing that this could be grounds for a long prison sentence. But he did as he was ordered and when finished, he signed the document. He felt he had little to lose at this point, and just wanted to get out of this terrible place.

The official and guards took the statement and left the room, leaving him alone again. Josef felt even more frightened as he waited for things to take their course. His mind ran wild at what could happen to him now.

One of the guards returned, pulling Josef up by one shoulder and said, "You had better go fast now. Get out of here before they change their minds and leave you here to rot."

Josef looked the guard in the eye. "Thank you," he said. "Thank you."

Taking the guard's advice, he left the barracks quickly on foot. The big black iron gates were open, and he walked out alone but free.

He felt a great relief, but he was aware that he was shaking all over and his recent beatings were still very painful. Even though he felt decidedly unwell, he began running as fast as he could down the road away from the dreaded barracks.

After a few minutes, he stopped running, took some deep breaths, and collapsed on the ground beneath his feet. He slowly dragged himself over to the side of the road and sat in the grass by a ditch utterly exhausted.

After resting awhile, he noticed that the ditch ran adjacent to the road. Beyond it, just a meter or so away, was a wide, fast flowing river that he guessed was the Elbe. He jumped into the ditch and crawled down the bank to the other side towards the river where he once more collapsed to his knees on the grassy bank. He laid his few personal possessions on the ground beside him, and began to wash his injuries. As he did so, he didn't realise that he was slowly slipping down the muddy bank into the river.

Before he knew what was happening, he was in the river and could feel the strong current pulling him along and down. He panicked, as he couldn't swim very well. No matter what he tried to do, the current pulled him further out into the centre of the deep, wide river. Struggling to keep afloat, he saw houses rush by him on the opposite bank. He screamed for help but nobody heard him. Suddenly he saw a bend in the river. The current pulled him closer to the far bank where he crashed into a fallen tree trunk lying partly on the bank and protruding out into the river. He screamed with pain as his whole body took the full force of the blow. But he was able to hang onto the tree as the river flowed past him at great speed.

It took tremendous willpower as well as strength to pull himself onto the fallen trunk and then struggle along it until he reached dry land and safety. His first thought was that he was safe and the second was that all his worldly possessions, his little wrap of memories, were on the other side of the river downstream somewhere. Although he was exhausted and soaking, he started back crossing a bridge, on his way to where he had gone into the river. It took him more that an hour. Thankfully, all of his cherished possessions were still where he had left them. He gave a deep sigh of relief and said a little prayer.

As he sat in the ditch, he opened his little cloth pack and there, safe and sound, were his chess pieces and his little statue of the Madonna and the piece of coal. These were reminders of his terrible time in Russia over the last ten years, but they were also reminders that he had survived not only that ordeal but also this current one. He was finally heading home with a few small gifts for his family. While he was collecting his senses and trying to regain his strength, a delivery truck that had just left the barracks, pulled up alongside him.

"Where you going, Comrade?" said the cheerful driver.

"To Bavaria," Josef replied.

"Hop in, if you like. I can take you as far as Karl-Marx-Stadt.

"Where?" enquired Josef.

The driver repeated his destination. "I have been away for awhile," Josef said. "Where is that?"

"You probably know it as Chemnitz which it was until this lot took over."

"This lot?" Josef asked.

The driver introduced himself as Bruno and said he came from Karl-Marx-Stadt.

This government that we have are Communists. Don't get me wrong," he continued somewhat defensively. "I have nothing against them but they do what the Soviets tell them to do. We are not free like in the West. Our government here is just a puppet of the Soviet Union."

"Oh, right! I understand," replied Josef in a reassuring way. "And yes, I would like to take up your kind offer of a ride to Karl-Marx-Stadt." They both exchanged smiles.

The journey took about forty-five minutes during which time the pair chatted amicably, mainly about the East German government and its failure to be able to keep its population from leaving the country and moving to the West.

"Here they call themselves the German Democratic Republic," Bruno told Josef.

"If you need to call yourselves democratic then you probably aren't," Josef joked, and they both laughed.

Josef enquired what Bruno had done in the war. "I was mostly in the West," he said. "I was lucky. Belgium, France! There was lots of champagne, wine and women. In fact, we had no problems until the invasion in '44. I was in France at the time. It was chaos. The Allies came in such strength that nothing was going to stop them. It was the beginning of the end for us. Then I was injured in the Battle of the Bulge. Look!" Bruno took his left hand off the wheel and showed Josef his arm. It had a massive scar on it. "Shrapnel!" he said. "I was out for weeks. Out of the fray I mean! They took me to a field hospital in Luxembourg. It took some time to recover and, by that time the war was nearly over. I was taken prisoner by the Americans. They weren't too bad. At least they fed us! How about you?"

Josef gave a shortened version of his time in the army and his imprisonment. By the time he had finished, it was getting late and they were arriving in Karl-Marx-Stadt in the district of Hilbersdorf. Bruno turned to Josef and asked him where he would be staying that night.

Josef replied that he wasn't sure. "Stay with us then? You are very welcome." Josef thanked him for his hospitality, and said that he would be grateful for a place to stay.

Bruno parked the vehicle outside his tenement apartment, and they went up to the fourth floor where he and his wife lived. Once inside the cosy home, Bruno introduced his wife Magda to Josef. She was a short, plump, red-faced, homely-looking woman of about 35 wearing a white apron pulled tightly around her waist. Bruno explained Josef's position to his wife, and she was pleased to agree to let Josef stay the night. She shook Josef's hand and enquired whether the pair had eaten? They both shook their heads and in no time at all they were both tucking into a plate of sauerkraut and delicious pork cutlets washed down by a beer each.

Josef was now really tired and after a bed was made up for him for the night on a settee in the sitting room, he got in and quickly fell sound asleep. He slept well and dreamed of home. He was roused from his sleep early the next morning, just as it was getting light, by a hammering on the front door of the apartment.

"Who the hell is that?" Bruno called out as he made his way to the door in his long johns.

"Police! Open up!" Josef heard all this but stayed silent in bed leaving the problem to Bruno. When Bruno opened the door, the police poured in, six of them in all.

"My God! It's the Stasi! What do you want at this time of the morning?" Bruno asked with some fear in his voice.

"You were seen arriving in your truck late last night by a neighbour who said you had a stranger with you. Who was he?" the officer demanded.
Bruno knew the East German Security Police, known as the Stasi, by reputation and knew that they were to be feared.

"He is an ex German prisoner of war of the Soviets returning home after many years in their prisons," Bruno explained, coming to Josef's defence. "And he was asleep in there," he said pointing to the sitting room. "Bet he isn't sleeping now!"

The guards charged into the sitting room to find Josef still in bed. "Get up," the officer shouted. "Get dressed! You are coming with us." Josef did as he was ordered. Rough treatment was second nature to him by now. As he was marched out between two guards, he thanked Bruno for his hospitality.

"I hope for your sake, Josef, you are who you say you are," Bruno said with some disappointment, doubt and fear in his voice.

"I am! Bruno, I am. Please have no fear of that," Josef insisted.
The police bundled Josef into a car and drove to the local Stasi headquarters some distance away. There he was strip-searched and interrogated for several hours.

Before he was allowed to leave Stasi headquarters, he had to sign a document to the effect that during his time as a prisoner of the Soviet Union he had been treated well. This Josef did just to get out of the place. Then he was ordered to leave.

"And don't come back, the policeman shouted at him. You are not wanted here in the GDR."

Josef left Stasi HQ mid-morning and immediately saw a road sign to Plauen, seventy kilometres west.

He decided that it would be his next stop. He felt deeply saddened as he left the city, let down and disappointed by the reception he had received in his own homeland, a homeland he had fought for during six terrible years of war. It certainly had not been what he had expected.

Chapter Thirteen - Shot on the Border

The sun was shining on his back as Josef left Karl-Marx-Stadt hoping that the worst was behind him as he got ever nearer to his home. After about an hour of walking along a small lane towards Zwickau, a car screeched to a halt alongside him and stopped.

"Want a lift, Comrade?" said a debonair, smartly dressed man of about 40. He was wearing a light grey, expensive-looking, fitted suit and was driving a sleek, black Mercedes with cream-covered leather seats.

"That would be very kind," Josef said, as he hurriedly opened the door and got it.

"Where are you going?" the stranger asked. Before Josef could answer the question, the driver told him that he was from Stuttgart in West German and his name was Wolfgang Schumacher. He said that he had been on a business trip to Dresden.

"I hope it was successful," Josef replied.

"Oh, I think so. Who knows though before the first orders start coming in? These Commies over here drive hard bargains you know."

Josef finally got a word in. "I have been a prisoner in the Soviet Union since the end of the war and am now on my way home."

"That's a long time to be away from home," Wolfgang said with a frown on his face.

"It is, and now I just want to get back to my family and farm in Bavaria," he replied.

"Let's see how far I can take you then," Wolfgang replied, as his frown turned into a smile.

Josef thanked him, as he settled down on the luxurious leather seat. The car was warm inside and within moments, he dozed off as the car sped on at great speed, quickly passing Zwickau as they headed west. While Josef slept, he dreamed of his journey to Bayreuth in the back of a truck on the day he had joined the army. Did that all really happen to him so long ago? The whole experience of the last sixteen years had been one long nightmare.

Josef was woken suddenly from his sleep by the screeching of brakes, and the shouts of the driver as the beautiful, black Mercedes left the road, turned over twice, and came to a standstill in a cornfield.

"Oh my car, my beautiful car," sobbed Wolfgang, not seeming to care whether Josef was dead or alive.

"But we are okay, and that is the most important thing, isn't it?" Josef asked.

"Yes, but my car is ruined! I will be sacked! I can't believe it! Can't you say it was your fault?" he begged Josef.

"What? You must be joking! I was sleeping and had nothing to do with the accident."

"Then you had better get out and go, as I am not really allowed to carry passengers," Wolfgang whined.

Josef did as he was told. "Are you sure you are not hurt, Wolfgang?" Josef stopped to ask.

"Yes, yes, just go!" Wolfgang repeated, his whole body shaking with shock.

Josef got out of the battered, mud-splattered car, thanked Wolfgang again for the lift saying he hoped he would be able to resolve his present situation successfully. Still a bit shaken himself, he continued to head west on foot, leaving Wolfgang to his own devises.

It was not long before he reached Plauen, a pretty town on the Elster River, which he had visited many times before when he was young. His uncle and aunt had lived there.

He wondered if they had survived the war. They had owned an inn known as The Pension Schmidt just outside the town. Walking through the town, he found the place quite easily, although he hadn't been there for twenty years or more. When he arrived, nothing outwardly seemed to have changed. The place looked just the same, neat and tidy with lots of geraniums in tubs outside. He entered the bar and immediately in front of him cleaning a table, stood his Aunt Christa, a portly lady in her late sixties. She looked up but didn't recognise Josef at first. When she looked a second time, she reacted with shock and amazement.

"Josef? Josef Holz?" she whispered. "It is you! It is you! My God, we thought you were." She stopped in mid sentence somewhat embarrassed, not wanting to say the word.

Tears came to Josef's eyes as he embraced her. She seemed somewhat cold toward him, and didn't really return his embrace warmly although she did say how pleased she was to see him. She pulled herself away from his embrace saying, "Your Uncle Klaus died in the war, Josef. Did you know? We don't know what happened to him. He just never came back."

Josef shook his head and listened quietly to the news that his uncle had been killed because of the horrible war. Now it was even more personal as Klaus was his late father's younger brother. Had his father been alive and had not died of cancer in

192

his own bed before the war began, then he too might have died in the war. Josef thought that at least his father had a grave. His Aunt Christa had nothing, just memories.

"I am so sorry, Aunt Christa. He was a fine man. That must have been awful for you what with the children to raise on your own and this place to run. Don't you know anything about what happened to him or where he is buried?"

"There is nothing," she replied with tears streaming down her puffy red cheeks. "He was just one of the millions of brave German soldiers who never came back. And when I asked the authorities if they knew what had happened to him, I was told there was no report of his death and no known grave."

Josef tried to comfort her by placing his arm around her shoulder, but she remained cold toward him, and could not be pacified.

"As well as losing my dear Klaus," she continued, " my brother Edgar also perished. He was killed in Russia. At least he has a grave even if it is somewhere in Russia where no one will ever visit. Thankfully he is also now remembered on a stone memorial in Mödlareuth in Bavaria where he lived before the war, not far from your place in Sparneck."

"I am so sorry," Josef repeated, stumbling over his words. He had not known her brother Edgar, but he was sure he was a fine man, a true son of Bavaria. He felt for his Aunt Christa; he felt her pain. He understood.

"What about your family in Königsberg? You had a sister, didn't you? How is she? Josef enquired.

Overcome with sorrow, his aunt sat down on an old wooden stool nearby and continued to sob. Josef realised he shouldn't have asked the question but it was too late now.

After awhile she stood up, dried her eyes and replied. "My dear Traudl, my baby sister." She stopped speaking for a few minutes, composed herself, and continued. "She never got out of the city. In 1944, the people of Königsberg got wind of the terrible atrocities being carried out on German civilians by the Soviets. The city was under siege for three months and thousands perished. From what I learned later," she continued, "there was a temporary German breakout allowing many civilians to escape on trains and ships. These were under constant bombardment and resulted in many deaths. What happened to Traudl, I will never know.

As a family," she continued tearfully, "we paid a very high price in the awful wars and there are now three names from our families on that memorial in Mödlareuth. Klaus's and Edgar's in the Second World War and Klaus's father in the First World War. How much do we have to give as a family to live in peace?" She asked raising both hands in despair.

Josef had no answer for her, but tried to move on by asking after his own family in Sparneck. His aunt thought for a moment then said that she had not seen Josef's wife, Helma, for years. "With these two German States it is not easy to travel back and forth over the border," she explained. "The authorities on this side do not encourage it, and the questioning and threats are awful. It just puts me off going. I am so sorry Josef, that I have nothing to tell you." Saying that he certainly understood, he asked her how she was keeping.

With a deep sigh, she continued. "Eight years after the end of the war when Klaus hadn't returned, and I hadn't heard from him, I was able to have him legally certified as 'presumed dead.' This allowed me to marry again. It wasn't for love, Josef, but Alfried, my new husband, is a good man and works hard at the business. I am now Christa Rathmann. Mrs Holz died with her husband in the war," she said blowing her nose.

Josef fondly told her how happy he was to see her safe and well after all the years that had passed, and he promised her that they must keep in touch. "Now, Aunt Christa, I need to continue my journey home. I am almost there."

"After all this time, Josef, do you think I would let you go without feeding you?" she said with a hint of her old smile on her face. Josef smiled back, sat down and relaxed while his aunt busied herself in the kitchen.

When she returned, she was carrying a meal on a tray, but Josef was asleep. "Hey! Wake up, Sleepy Head," she said with a smile.

Josef opened his eyes and smiled back at her. "Thank you, Aunt Christa."

Taking the tray from her, he found a bowl of piping hot goulash, black bread and a beer.

"What is this, Aunt, Harvest Festival?" he joked. She ran the fingers of her right hand through his soft greying hair affectionately and said, "you deserve it, my boy. I can't imagine what you have been through over the last years?" Feeling comforted at last by his aunt's show of kindness, Josef began eating the delicious meal. When he finished, he dozed off again for a short time before standing up and embracing her.

"Thank you so much for the marvellous food and rest, Aunt. I cannot begin to tell you how much it has meant to me to be with you even for such a short time. It has been a blessing for me to have found you have survived after all these years of horror."

"It is ok, Josef. I am so happy to see you again and to know that you too survived the nightmare." She embraced him, and this time Josef felt real warmth and affection.

"Maybe now you are back, I will make a trip to the West to see you if I can get a pass," she said, adding, "Give my love to Helma and the boys. Don't forget now!"

Josef said that it would be wonderful for her to visit. "Mind you," he warned, "I don't yet know myself how things may have changed at home, whether my family is still there or whether Helma has remarried." He went quiet for a moment thinking what he had just said. Could that be possible? He hadn't really thought about it before. He just assumed everything would be the same as when he had left all those years ago as though time had just stood still. Now the possibilities flooded into his mind, and he was worried.

They wished each other "Auf Wiedersehen," kissing each other on both cheeks and holding each other tightly for a moment.

After he left his aunt, he was pensive and brooding as he headed back into town. All their lives had been changed so much by the war, and nothing would be the same as it had been before he went away. He now realised that his mistake had been thinking that he was the only one that the war had affected. He hadn't considered those he had left behind. He felt ashamed to have thought that everything would have remained the same. The war had had a cataclysmic effect on the entire German nation, yet he had only focused on himself and those immediately around him during the war.

He reached the centre of the town and saw that there was a bus that was going to Hof, in Bavaria, which was not far from his home. He spoke to the driver who said that the journey took about two hours and cost 10 marks. Josef got on and paid his fare from the little he had left from Tomasz's generosity. Once he had paid his money, the driver turned to Josef and said, "You will not be allowed to cross the border at Gassenreuth unless you have the correct papers."

"Correct papers?" Josef asked.

"Yes! You must leave the bus if you don't have the right papers," the bus driver said, adding, "You need an exit visa to leave East Germany."

Josef decided he would take the bus anyway. At least it was going in the right direction and he had already paid. After all, he did have his crumpled release paper from the prison camp. Hopefully this would be enough.

It was a pleasant afternoon as the bus pulled away from the stop on the last stage of his journey home. They passed many pretty villages as he admired the beautiful green, hilly, Saxon countryside and dreamed of being home at last.

The bus arrived at the village of Posseck with its ancient church. Nobody got on or off the bus there, and it soon pulled away with a jolt for Gassenreuth, the border village. The border between the two Germanys was a mile or so west of this village on the road to the next village, Gattendorf, in Bavaria. It was the border between Saxony and Bavaria, the border between two States and two ideologies. Suddenly, Josef panicked and decided to get off the bus. Perhaps the driver had been correct. He just couldn't face being questioned again by the East German Border Police.

He waited until the bus had departed and, as inconspicuously as possible, started walking toward the small hamlet of Gattendorf, about two miles away.

In normal times, the walk between the two villages would have taken around half an hour on the road. This time, however, he decided to cross through the fields between the villages. All the time his heart was pounding out loud, or so it seemed.

He thought it was ridiculous that as a German he could not cross the border freely, but if this was what it took to avoid confrontation, he would have a go. After all, he had come so far and he was now so near to his home.

He walked out of the hamlet, climbed over a fence and began to cross a field of corn. There wasn't anything there to show that he was crossing any border but he did see a small stream, and he knew the village ahead, beyond the trees, was Gattendorf. Local knowledge was a good thing, and he had grown up in these parts. 'Growing up,' he thought. That was another world away; he just wasn't the same person. So much had happened since his idyllic childhood.

He saw the woods ahead of him, but as he approached them he heard shouting coming from behind.

"Stop, you cannot proceed any further. We must check your papers."

Josef turned and looked back. He saw two soldiers climbing over a fence in pursuit of him with machine guns slung over their backs. He acted as though he hadn't heard the order and continued walking. Soon his walking quickened and then he began to run as fast as he could.

"Stop, or I will fire!" Josef heard the order and the click of a rifle behind him as it was loaded and a bullet entered the chamber ready to fire. He ran faster in the hope of making the cover of the woods.

He next heard the report of the rifle, and he was immediately thrown forward onto the earth as a bullet penetrated his right shoulder. He screamed out in pain as he felt warm blood oozing from a wound on the right side of his upper chest. He lay there motionless on the damp Saxon soil as he heard running feet coming up behind him.

"Is he dead?" asked one.

"Doesn't look like it," said the other adding, "but does it matter? I think he is a criminal trying to escape to the West. Anyway we had better get him back to base." Josef heard all this as if from far away as he lapsed into unconsciousness. It seemed that his luck had finally run out. He had come so far, so near to home, and yet a million miles from sanity.

At the scene, the guards provided some basic first aid to stop the bleeding, but it was a while before his limp body was picked up, put on a stretcher and taken in an ambulance to the local hospital back in Plauen where his condition was described as satisfactory. He had lost a lot of blood, but his injuries were not thought to be life threatening.

Eventually, the Stasi interviewed him. In fact, he was interviewed a number of times from his hospital bed, but each time his story was the same. It was the truth, but the Stasi didn't understand that people sometimes tell the truth. They dealt in lies and deception and the truth was alien to them.

It was three weeks before he was allowed to leave the hospital with two big hospital orderlies escorting him directly to the local Stasi offices.

He was once again interviewed, this time by a Bavarian Stasi officer who had chosen to live under the Communists in Saxony. Josef played along with him and chatted about Bavaria and his own family in Sparneck, a town the officer said he knew well.

"I just want to get home to my wife and family," Josef explained. "That is if they are still there. I have had no contact with them since the end of the war."

The officer said he understood and Josef would be allowed to leave the DDR but would have to sign a document to the effect that he had been shot accidentally on a hunting trip. Josef agreed. He would have agreed to anything, if it meant he could leave the Stasi offices and get to Bavaria.

The following day, after a night in a cell, the Bavarian Stasi officer collected Josef and drove him to a place near to the spot where he had been shot in the field three weeks earlier. It seemed a lifetime ago. It was a bright, warm day and the sun shone from a clear blue sky.

"You are free! Good luck in the West," said the Stasi officer and that was it. He was gone. Before

Josef could even shake his hand and thank him, he had walked back to his car and driven off.

Like in a time warp, Josef remembered the last time he had stood at this spot. He remembered seeing the trees ahead, of running with his heart pounding in his chest, and hearing the shot and falling to the ground. Now he just walked across the field where he had walked three weeks earlier toward Gattendorf and real freedom.

Chapter Fourteen - Homecoming

Josef headed off from Gassenreuth where he had been shot, and soon found the road to Gattendorf. He walked toward the Bavarian village and freedom. Some distance before he arrived in the village, a friendly West German border guard met him.

"Where are you going Friend? Or should I ask where have you been?" the officer asked Josef.

"How long do you have Officer? It might take some time to tell you," Josef replied with a smile.

The border guard smiled back at him, and said that he would take him to the police station in Hof to make a statement first and, then, if Josef agreed, go to the local hospital for a check up. Josef agreed even though he knew it would delay his return home.

He sat in the front seat of the police car beside the driver, enjoying the beautiful Franconian countryside that he knew so well. Within half an hour, he found himself at the police station in Hof where he made a short statement as to how he had come to be found crossing the border between East and West Germany.

After finishing with the paperwork, and within an hour of entering the police station, he was on his way to the hospital in a police car. When he arrived, Josef was surprised by how modern and friendly the hospital was, not at all like the one in Plauen. After a thorough medical examination, the doctor told him he was very lucky to have survived the shooting. "An inch or so to the right," the doctor said, "would have severed a main artery, and you would not be here now to tell us your story." Once more Josef realised how lucky he was despite his many ordeals and delays.

After Josef's medical examination, he had a beautiful bath after which the hospital provided him with a good lunch and a comfortable bed to sleep in. It seemed a miracle to lie under crisp white bedding and listen to the radio, which was playing softly in the background. He slept well that night at the hospital, but in the morning he became agitated and wanted to be off as soon as possible. After a few more tests, he was told that considering his ordeal, he was in remarkably good health. Josef ate another lunch at the hospital, and napped for a short while before waking suddenly feeling ready to be on his way. He thanked the doctor and staff for their care and attention and left in the late afternoon.

As he walked down the steps of the hospital, he took a deep breath. He had come home at last. The streets of Hof were very familiar to him, as he made his way through the town toward Sparneck, which was only a short distance south of the town.

He had walked for only a few minutes when he heard a car approach. He hailed the car and when it stopped, he asked the driver, an elderly gentleman dressed in a Bavarian grey jacket and lederhosen, if he were going in the direction of Sparneck.

"Of course I am. Climb aboard!" Josef grinned and got in. Within a few minutes, they arrived in the centre of the small, market town of Münchberg. Josef gratefully thanked the driver, and told him that he wanted to continue the last kilometre or so of his journey on foot. Feeling both anxiety and anticipation, he began to make his way toward Sparneck and home. As he passed the railway station he glanced over the road and saw where the Goldstein's had been. It was now boarded up and derelict. Josef wondered if they had been caught up in the terrible war.

His home was just outside the little town of Sparneck, in a small group of farmhouses known as Grosslosnitz. His family had lived there for generations. It truly was home and Josef knew every brick in the old building where he had grown up.

By the time he reached the cluster of familiar farmhouses, it was already getting dark. There was a full moon, and as he made his way from the main road up the rough track, he saw his white, three-storey home with the little attic window above. He had made it! He had come home! He noticed that the lights were on in the sitting room and the kitchen.

Suddenly, he began to panic. What if his family had moved? What if they hadn't survived the war? What if Helma had remarried? His head was swimming in doubt and questions.

He ran the last few metres up to the front door and just stood there frozen. Thoughts flooded through his mind about the last years. In an instant, he remembered all that had happened to him in the war: his capture, his imprisonment, and finally his perilous journey home. Now he stood at the front door of his home. He felt an overwhelming sense of relief, but he could not bring himself to knock on the door. It was his own front door, but he couldn't knock on it.

To actually have made it home, brought tears to his eyes, and he began to sob quietly. He knew he couldn't knock on the door while he was so upset, so he went into the barn at the back of the house. There he lay down on a bale of hay, and within a few moments was asleep. Exhaustion and relief had taken their toll. He slept deeply, a sleep of release that he was at his journey's end. He rested well and long that night not waking until late into the morning. The sun was high in the clear blue sky, and it was another gorgeous day.

He lay there listening to the familiar sounds around him: chickens cackling, cows mooing, a dog barking in the distance, and birds singing. These were the sounds he had known all his life and in his darkest times had longed to hear once more.

The smell of nature, a farm smell, good and rich and deep confirmed he was home. He remembered playing hide and seek with his father and romping in the hay with his mother in this very barn when he was young. It had always seemed a homely, fresh, clean place to him.

Then he began to wonder how his family would receive him after such a long time away, if, indeed, they were still there. He began to panic again. He jumped off the straw bale and washed in running cold water from a tap that protruded through the wall in the corner. When he had dried himself on a piece of sacking, he looked into a broken piece of mirror, which he found on a ledge. What he saw surprised him. He did not recognise himself under so much hair, even after his clean up at the hospital. Anyway, he thought that he looked as well as he was going to look until his hair was cut. He licked his fingers and ran them through his hair trying to arrange it better, but to no avail. He had put off long enough knocking on the front door. He took three deep breaths smelling the fresh Franconian air.

Once again he started shaking as he walked to the front door and knocked. There was a long delay; at least it seemed a long delay, before the door opened. There stood Helma, a little older, a little broader, but there she was. She looked deeply at his face with shocked, enquiring eyes. It was a long look, a searching look, a look with a million questions and no answers. She took a step backward, put her hands up to her face and collapsed onto her knees crying, "My God! My God!"

Rushing towards her, Josef also dropped to his knees, and they both cried quietly in each other's arms. They hugged each other and their hands stroked each other's faces in wonder. With the back of his hand, Josef felt her still beautiful face as she lovingly explored his beard and hair, running her fingers around his eyes, nose and lips. They kissed each other deeply, yearning to reconnect with their hearts and their bodies. She was still totally desirable to him, this woman he had waited so many years for, the women who had given him two beautiful sons and the strength to carry on, and to endure those years of war and captivity.

To her, he was the man she would never accept had been lost in the war. She always knew that one day he would come back to her. There were many occasions when she could have had him declared, "presumed dead," but she had never even considered it. She had always thought that she had her two sons, and knew that she had her husband, their father, wherever he was, she was confident that one day he would return.

When they had recovered from the initial shock of the reunion, Helma said "Come! I will run a bath for you." But after looking carefully at him again, she added with a smile, "I think I had better feed you first."

Josef thankfully sat down in his easy chair, which still stood in the corner by the window. He just relaxed and closed his eyes. He smelt the mouth-watering aroma of bacon sizzling in the pan, bread toasting and coffee brewing.

Soon Helma called from the kitchen. "It's ready, Josef! Come! Eat!" There were eggs, bacon, ham, toast and the most delicious coffee on the table before him. It was beautiful and Josef ate and drank till he could eat and drink no more. At the back of his mind were his meals with Anna, and the nights. He would tell Helma one day. He knew he had to, needed to, but now was not the time. It could wait.

"Where are my boys?" he asked, as she stood behind him massaging his neck and shoulders. She still couldn't really believe that her beloved husband was finally home. All she wanted was to be close to him, to touch him, to cling to him, to make love with him.

"Herman is seventeen and at farming college in Hof. Siegfried is nineteen now and has a driving job. He is sometimes away for days," she said adding with a smile on her face, "which gives me time to clear up his mess! They are both very good though around the farm and help out so much. I couldn't manage this place without their help." Josef grinned with pride, finished his breakfast and stood up. He kissed his wife on the forehead and then the lips again.

"Come, the bath water should be ready by now," said Helma as she led her darling husband to the bathroom and slowly undressed him. He stood there before her naked and felt how good it was. She was saddened by how gaunt and ravaged he had become over the past years, but what she saw was hers and only hers. They both felt that way.

Once Josef was in the bath and lying in the gloriously hot water, Helma gently washed his thin, weary body as though washing out all the filth, the obscenities, and the degradation of the years he had been away. His bad feelings began slipping away as he lay in the bath and was washed clean by the most beautiful woman in the world. In fact, he wasn't really dirty, as he had bathed in the hospital in Hof the day before. This was more a ritual bathing, a cleansing of mind and body.

When she finished, Josef stood up, and she dried him as he felt his masculinity coming to life. He put on his eldest son's dressing gown, which Helma offered him, and they went into the bedroom. There on the wall he saw a large plate that showed the Alps and a little house half way up the mountain. On the bottom rim of the plate on a scroll were the words "Hitler's Bauhaus." His mother had given them the plate of the fuehrer's farmhouse before the war as a Christmas gift. Seeing it now, Josef laughed. "You still have that awful plate, Helma?"

She smiled, "Your mother gave it to us."

"Perhaps it is time to take it down!" he said. "And smash it! It is the past and a horrible one, at that. Oh, and by the way," Josef continued, "I noticed the Goldstein's shop was boarded up. What happened to them?"

"I don't know Josef. They say that one night the whole family were arrested by the Gestapo and were never seen again. After the war we heard that they had been sent east where they perished. It was awful, awful for everyone. You know," she continued, "it was a terrible time for the German people under the Nazis. There was always a feeling that at any time you might be arrested for the slightest thing. The whole nation lived in fear." Josef frowned but stayed silent. What could he say about the flood of hate the war had brought?

He slowly removed his dressing gown and got into bed. Helma took off her clothes and joined him. They made love as if nothing in the world mattered, and at that moment, truly, nothing did. They gave themselves to each other as though trying to make up for the past, the lost years, but they both knew that in reality it was not possible.

They were happy, as they both knew that they were still very much in love with each other. They also knew that no matter what, neither of them had ever given up hope that one day they would see each other again, and be together.

"I always knew you would come back some day, Josef," Helma said. "I never gave up hope."

"I, too, knew that this day would come," he agreed. "It is what sustained me, and gave me the strength to carry on. It is why I woke up every day. Without the hope that one day I would get back to you and the boys, I would have given up years ago and put an end to my wretched life."
Helma looked into his eyes and said, "I love you Josef, completely."

"As I love you," he replied reassuringly putting his arm around her naked body and kissing her deeply on the lips, her neck, working his way down to her body to her middle where he lingered with his tongue caressing her soft, willing body. He felt her pushing toward him, meeting him fully.

After their beautiful love making, they just lay there looking at each other incredulous that they were actually together again. After what seemed an eternity, they dressed and went downstairs to the sitting room. Once more they could not stop looking at each other. It was almost as if time had stopped and the intervening years had never happened.

Josef found his little backpack that he had carried with him for so many months, and took out the small wooden figure of the Madonna. He gave it to his wife who was snuggled up beside him. "It's for you, my darling. I made it for you."

She looked at it and kissed it. "Thank you, Josef! I will treasure this as long as I live, but more importantly, I have you. You are my treasure." Just then they heard the front door open.

"That will be Siegfried. He's early today," she said looking at the clock on the mantelpiece. They continued sitting together holding hands in front of the large window of the sitting room as the late afternoon sun flooded in from behind them.

As Siegfried entered the room, he saw the unfamiliar figure and stood motionless just looking, questioning. "Hallo! Who are you then?" he asked.

Siegfried was a handsome, tall young man with a pale complexion, long golden blond hair, and deep blue eyes. He worked as a truck driver for a local company. Josef could see he was the mirror image of himself when he was the same age.

"This is your father, Sigi. He has come back to us," Helma said to her son, who just stood there transfixed, staring at Josef. Siegfried then noticed that tears of joy were running down his mother's cheeks.

Without a word, Siegfried crossed the room and stood close beside his father. Josef felt his son's fingertips run through his hair several times.

"I have always wanted to do that to my father," Siegfried said, his voice breaking with emotion. Josef turned a little and buried the side of his face in his son's chest as he wrapped his arms around his son's thin body. Arms around each other, they wept silently together for several minutes. Taller than his father, Sigi's rested the side of his face on his father's head. Nothing was said. They just enjoyed the closeness of each other after so many years apart. They both knew that they had missed too much of each other's love over the years, but now they were together again and things would be different.

"The last thing I remember about you, Son, is reading you the story of Pinocchio. Silly really as you were only a baby, but I wanted you to hear my voice. It always seemed to settle you down. I remember hearing my father's voice reading the same book to me when I was young. It was by Carlo Collochi, an Italian, about a little wooden boy puppet whose nose grew when he told lies. In fact it was an original book from the 1880s. I wonder where it is? It belonged to my grandmother. It must be quite valuable by now?"

"It is still up in the cupboard, Josef," Helma volunteered.

Josef smiled and remembered. He jumped up and looked in the cupboard. Sure enough! There was the book. He took it from the shelf and ran his fingers over the cover. He opened the book and looked inside and there was his grandmother's name Viktoria Emma Holz. He ran his fingers over the name and felt that for the first time in many years his life was complete. He had his family again.

He handed the book to Siegfried, "It is yours son. Take it. This is your heritage." Siegfried took the book in both hands and kissed it. "Thank you Father. I will treasure it." Sitting back down on the settee, next to his father, he was amazed! It was incredible! He had a father at last. His father had returned home from the war.

A little later, as the sun was disappearing behind the hill, they heard the front door open. All three of them knew it was Herman, and they sat there waiting for him to burst into the room. Herman was attending a course at the local Farming College in Hof where he commuted daily on his moped. Without even glancing into the sitting room, he called out "Hi, mum," and went straight up to his room. The three of them exchanged glances, all wondering what they should do now.

Helma called up the stairs that she had a surprise for him, and he should come back down, but he shouted down that he had so much homework it might be a while before he could have his dinner.

Siegfried, who was holding one of his father's hands, said that he would go up and explain things to his brother adding, "Herman can be difficult when he wants to be. He missed not having a father the most. He never knew you. He is not very sure of himself and never has been." Siegfried stood up and left the room. Josef could hear his footsteps as he climbed the sixteen stairs.

Some time elapsed before there was movement on the stairs again. Siegfried re-entered the room and said simply "He said that he doesn't believe me, that I am lying and that his father is dead, killed in the war like every other kid's father around here."

Josef stood up, "Well, I wasn't killed. I survived and I will go up and tell him so."

Picking up his little bundle from the settee, he excused himself from their company, ran his hand through Siegfried's beautiful, shiny blonde hair, and stroked his wife's face before leaving the room. He slowly mounted the stairs that led to the bedrooms on the first floor. Herman's room was at the front of the house facing east. It had been his own room when he was young.

He knocked on his son's door and waited. Getting no response, he entered the room uninvited. Herman was lying on his bed facing the wall away from his father. "Herman, I am your father. When I last saw you and held you in my arms, you were a beautiful baby. Your mother and I made two beautiful babies. Now you are both beautiful, grown men, my sons, and I am so proud of you both. I am so sorry I could not be here for you as you grew up. You have never known my love in person, but I swear to you now, Son, that not a day passed over all the years I was away, that I didn't think of you, your brother and your wonderful mother.

My only fear was that if ever I were released and made it home, you might not be here and that I would not be able to find you. But Herman, I always believed that one day I would find my family again. It was with this knowledge that I would see you again, that I was able to carry on for so long. I survived because of you."

Josef had the feeling that perhaps he had said too much and had not given Herman a chance to explain his feelings. "We have the rest of our lives to show how we feel, Son, and tonight may be too soon."

Herman turned over and looked directly into his father eyes. "Most of us kids around here have no fathers. They were all killed in the war. At least, you have come home now. Really, I am happy for us all. It is just that this is all so hard to take in."

"I would never have gone away if I could have helped it, Son. I was a farmer. I tended cows and grew corn. I wasn't cut out to shoot guns and kill Russians. None of us were. Do you think that any of us in my battalion wanted to be there? We didn't! None of those I knew, and we were all conscripts, were political in any way or members of the Nazi party. There may have been some who were, but I didn't know them."

"I am glad you finally made it home, Father. I bet mum was pleased to see you?" he commented politely.

"Yes, of course she was Herman, very pleased. And shocked! And what about you? What do you think?" Josef enquired.

"I don't know yet. To finally have a father, it seems unreal."

Josef went to put his hand on his son's arm, but Herman moved away and stood up.
"Let's go down to dinner then," Herman said.

"Before you go downstairs, Herman, I have a little present for you. It's a chess set I made while I was a prisoner. I want you to have it."

Herman slowly took the pieces out of the cloth wrap as though to inspect them one by one. "They are beautiful, Father. Thank you. They must have taken you a long time to make?"

"I had a long time," Josef replied with a slight smile on his face.

Herman carefully wrapped the chess set up again in the cloth, and tucked them under his pillow, and indicated that they should go downstairs.

The others were waiting silently when Josef and Herman entered the room together. Josef saw that Helma had been crying again, and Siegfried's face was hidden in his hands with his elbows on the table. "All okay then?" Helma inquired, her voice near breaking with emotion.

"Yes! All okay, Mum," Herman replied, somewhat irritated by her question. Josef just gave his wife a blank look, which she did not know how to interpret, although she realised the meeting could not have been easy for either of them.

They ate the evening meal almost in silence as each member of the family dealt with the many thoughts and emotions of just being together again in their own separate ways.

That night Josef and Helma slept in each other's arms and it was beautiful. When they awoke in the morning, they called the boys who both came into their room and sat on either side of their bed enjoying the newness of being a family together at last. They discussed what they could do on their first day together as a family. It being a Saints Day and a holiday in Bavaria, Helma suggested that they should go to church. To Josef's surprise, both his sons agreed.

"Of course," said Herman, "We usually only go to church at Christmas and Easter, but it would be nice today, to sort of give thanks for your safe return."

Josef asked, "What about the cows. Have they been milked?" Even after all the years away from home, it seemed natural for him to ask that question.

"Oh course, Father, but that was at six this morning before any of you were awake," Siegfried said with a smile.

They all dressed in their Sunday clothes except Josef, as he didn't have any. He did, however, find a jacket and trousers tucked away in the wardrobe that still fitted him. He changed into them, borrowing one of Siegfried's white shirts and a tie. He looked a bit like a poor peasant but he didn't mind. He was home and he was going to give thanks to the Lord for bringing him safely back to his family.

Siegfried then went outside to harness the horse. While the others made themselves ready, he brought the trap around to the front of the house. They all climbed aboard and within a short time were on their way in warm sunshine to the church in Sparneck, about ten minutes away.

When they arrived at the church, Siegfried tied up the horse. Josef pushed open one of the two huge oak doors, waited a moment for Siegfried, and they entered the church as a family. Josef realised they were a bit late as he heard the organ music playing which signalled the beginning of the service. Josef felt waves of nostalgia rush through him as he remembered how he and Helma had been married here, and both his sons had been christened here. This church had played a central part in his life, and in the life of his parents and grandparents.

He had not been in the church for years, and had forgotten how beautiful it was. It was in the baroque style, an explosion of gold and white with religious, highly decorated wall paintings and statues everywhere. Angels, Madonnas, nymphs, crucifixes and stars all in gold, covered the walls and ceiling. It was overwhelmingly ornate and beautiful and light, and the organ played what Josef recognised as the Toccata and Fugue in D Minor by Bach as it had been a favourite of his father.

All the seats seemed to be taken as it was a special Saints day service, and Josef saw that the church was almost full to capacity. They slowly walked down the aisle past the congregation, all friends and neighbours. Josef and Helma were arm in arm in front with the two boys following side by side. When they were halfway down the aisle, Josef became aware that someone in the congregation had begun to clap, slowly at first but gradually getting faster and louder. Then another began clapping and another and another and another.

The congregation just burst into spontaneous applause, and then the cheering began overwhelming the little church and filling it with joy. The organ stopped abruptly as the organist also stood up, turned around with a smile on his face, and began clapping.

The priest, who was standing by the altar, looked up from his prayers at this unusual event and he too, upon seeing the family walking down the aisle, joined in with the clapping. Falling to his knees onto a little stool in front of him, he began praying.

Seats in the front row were quickly found for the family, as the applause died down. The priest looked at Josef and his family with tears in his eyes and said, "Let us pray." The whole congregation knelt and the priest began:

"Thank you, God. Thank God, for bringing our dear brother Josef home to us. It is a miracle on this our Saints Day, that the whole family stands here together before God, before me, and before the good people of this town after being apart for so long. I know it has been many years since they were all here together as a family. Thank you, dear Lord, Thank you!"

Tears ran down the faces of the family and, indeed, there were not many dry eyes in the whole church. Most remembered their own lost loved ones who had not returned from the war. Perhaps they could find hope that even now, after so many years, some of their loved ones might return as Josef had. He gave them all hope where there had been none. The congregation felt both happy and sad at the same time.

The priest then looked to Josef and asked if he would like to say a word. Josef shook his head. He was too emotional to speak. The priest then looked towards Helma who smiled, and stood up to speak.

"My dear family, friends and neighbours, this is the happiest day of my life. My Josef has come back to his family, whom he left so long ago. Looking back over the years, I don't know how I coped. I don't know how any of us survived loosing our men. At first we seemed so alone without them. Many of us didn't know whether they were alive or dead or if we would ever see them again.

I lived everyday as though it were my last because without my beloved Josef, I simply wanted it to be my last day. But I had two children who needed their mother, and this gave me a reason to carry on, to bear the unbearable. All through the years I never gave up hope that one day my beloved Josef would return to me. God is amazing and works in many wonderful ways. I believe it was the Lord who brought our community together to share our grief, and support each other during such terrible times, and that is what we did, and still do to this day. My message to you all is to never give up hope."

The priest nodded to Helma and then addressed the congregation. "We will now sing the hymn "Now Thank We All Our God." Josef tried but couldn't sing; he was so overwhelmed. He just listened to the healing words being sung by his family, friends, and neighbours and the sound of the thunderous organ filling the church on this very joyous occasion. After the service, there were hugs and hand shaking and tears from the congregation. All agreed that it was a miracle that Josef had returned.

On their journey back home after the service, except for the birds, it was quiet as Josef and his family enjoyed each other's company in silence. Once home, Helma said that she would prepare a late breakfast. Josef sat in the sitting room overcome by the events that had caught up with him. Shortly the whole family sat around their table, enjoying breakfast together for the first time. Josef asked if he might say a prayer before they ate, and after receiving nods all round he began:

"Dear Lord, thank you for returning me my family, my beautiful family, who have suffered so much over the years not having a husband and father to love and protect them. But, dear Lord, they always had your love. I was always comforted by the thought that You would keep them safe and they would be here when I returned. By your grace, we are now together again as a family. We thank You for this wonderful chance to get to know each other again."

At this point, Herman jumped up and left the room. Josef stood up to follow him outside but Helma stopped him.

"Leave him, Josef. Let him have some time on his own before you join him. He will want that." Josef understood that she knew her sons best, and obeyed her advice.

After about ten minutes, she nodded and Josef left the room to find his son. Outside, the air was warm and balmy even though the sun was temporarily hidden behind a fluffy cloud. He could hear his son in the barn crying, but he feared joining him in case he himself broke down again. This was the time when Herman needed a strong father to talk with him, to listen, to advise and understand.

He remembered the past when he was young. He would go to the back barn to be alone, when things sometimes went wrong between himself and his parents. So he waited a while longer before entering. His youngest son, his baby, was sitting on the bale of hay on which he himself had slept on his first night home. Herman's elbows were on his lap, and his hands covered his young, damp face. He looked up when his father entered the barn.

Their eyes met but neither said anything for a long moment. Once again, Josef put his hand on his son's arm, but this time his touch was not rejected. On the contrary, Herman took his father's hand in his and kissed it on the knuckle several times.

"In my dreams, Father, as a child, I always kissed my right hand last thing at night and said 'Good Night Father.' It was like kissing you each night. I wanted you to come back home one day to be with us. It seemed as if we never really lived without you; we survived without you, waiting for your return."

Tears began to run down Josef's face, and he couldn't control his emotions. He was embarrassed to be crying in front of his son but he couldn't help it. He stretched out his arms and embraced his beloved son.

"You have always been my hero, Father. Mother said that you were with us in thought even if you could not physically be here. We should always remember that and must be strong for you."

"And it was you, your mother, and your brother who sustained me all these years," replied Josef. Then Herman burst out saying, "In your prayer not once did you mention the terrible times you must have gone through. Were you tortured? Did they beat you? You must have been starving?"

"Hey, Hey, my darling boy," Josef interjected, holding Herman tightly in his arms resting the side of his face on his son's head. "So many questions and so many things to be answered, but not now. I didn't mention myself in the prayer because that is in the past, and we must plan for the future, a future with us as a family. Perhaps one day I will write a book of my adventures. What do you say? Will you help me?"

Herman looked at him curiously. "I was quite good at my German grammar, Father. I was top of the class. What would you call your book?"

Josef ran his fingers through his dear son's hair and said, "I guess it would be called something like 'Return From Russia.' What do you think?"

"That's a good title Father – simple and true. It is the story of your journey and how, against all the odds, you made it back home!"

"Yes, I did make the journey. And I am now home for good with my beloved family, and, I hope, with many years of happiness and peace before us all."

The End

Acknowledgements

My grateful thanks go to Mrs Maggie Colosimo of Denver, Colorado for reading the text and correcting my errors where necessary. Also her editorial comments and suggestions were invaluable in completing this book.

I would also like to thank my editor, Mrs Carole Murdock, and her husband John of Denver, Colorado for their enthusiastic help and support during the writing of this book.

Thanks also go to Russell Schooley and my daughter Hayley for their patience and understanding for the many hours I spent researching and writing during work time in the preparation of this book.

Finally my thanks to Sue Ransley for the beautiful cover artwork she produced for me.

**Josef's Wood Carving of the
Madonna and Child**